INK

HOUNDS OF HELLFIRE MC

FIONA DAVENPORT

Copyright © 2025 by Fiona Davenport

Cover designed by Elle Christensen

Edited by Jenny Sims (Editing4Indies)

All rights reserved.

No part of this book may be reproduced in any form or by any electronic or mechanical means, including information storage and retrieval systems, without written permission from the author, except for the use of brief quotations in a book review.

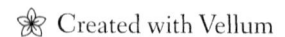

❀ Created with Vellum

INK

Matteo "Ink" DeLuca was born into the Mafia, but he chose a motorcycle club family instead. He was no stranger to commitment, but he'd never made one to a woman...until he met Annika Lee.

Annika's uncle was her only family. She never expected him to betray her. Or for the sexy tattoo artist to ride to her rescue.

PROLOGUE
INK

"*Che bella bambina! Una principessa!*" my *mamma* exclaimed, placing a hand dramatically on her chest. She gazed adoringly at the picture of the "princess" my aunt Bridget showed her on her phone.

The baby was Bridget's grandchild, Luna, who had just turned one. Since Bridget was actually my cousin—despite being old enough to be my mother—that made Luna some kind of cousin too, but I had so many of those, I'd stopped keeping track of how we were related.

We were Italian...baby making was in our blood. Or so my mother kept telling me.

My cousin Rafa leaned toward me and murmured, "Wait for it..."

I winced, knowing he was right, and sure enough, right on cue, my mother's watery eyes slid over to me.

"I would just love a grandbaby," she sighed. The sound alone sent a full-blown guilt trip square in my direction. A special talent most Italian mothers seemed to possess.

"*Mamma*," I muttered. "What exactly are Enzo and Valentina's kids, if not grandbabies?" My older brother and his wife had six kids, for the love of Sant'Anna. The Patron Saint of Mothers and Fertility was plenty busy with them.

"They live all the way up in New York City, Matteo," my mom responded with a sniff that was both sad and accusing at the same time.

"I'll get to it eventually," I grumbled. Though I seriously doubted it would be anytime soon.

She obviously knew me too well because she narrowed her eyes and snapped, "When?"

My mouth opened and closed a few times, and my eyes darted around, looking for an escape or help. Gavin, my sixteen-year-old brother, was grinning, and I glared, promising him retribution for enjoying my torture. At the head of the table, my stepfather, Alfonso, had his head down, seemingly focused on his food, but I could see the slight shake of his shoulders.

Almost twenty people were crammed into the dining room, and a little over half were men. The single guys were practically shrinking in their seats, trying to avoid being the next victim in the line of fire. And the married guys didn't even try to disguise how amused they found the whole spectacle.

Even Bridget's husband, Mac—the gruff president of the Silver Saints Motorcycle Club—who'd been like a second father to me and almost never smiled, had one corner of his mouth kicked up.

Bastards.

Finally, my eyes landed on Rafa, who sat next to me at the dinner table. My gaze slid away from him guiltily when I shrugged and said, "Rafa's older than me. Why don't you pester him about why he isn't married and making babies?"

If we hadn't been in my mom and stepfather's house, I probably would have felt the barrel of his gun in my ribs. Luckily for me, he didn't bring it to Sunday dinner. Well, not inside the house anyway.

"*Traditore*," he grunted.

Couldn't argue with that. I was definitely a traitor, but I'd do it again to save my own skin.

Aunt Giulia, Rafa's mother, snorted and shook

her head. "I've given up on Raffaele for grandbabies."

"Perhaps I simply haven't found the right woman," Rafa groused.

"And you never will if you don't stop working all the time and go on a date."

"I date," he defended himself half-heartedly.

"Taking your distant cousin to a charity ball last month hardly qualifies as a date, Rafa," Gabbi, his younger sister, chimed in with a delighted expression.

"How would you know?" he rebutted with a scowl. "You don't date."

She crossed her arms over her chest and glowered, "I could if you didn't scare away every man who even looks in my direction! And that's only if they aren't terrified by the last name DeLuca first."

"*Per amore di tutto ciò che è sacro*," Rafa sighed, looking up at the ceiling.

For the love of all that is holy is right, cuz. Where was a miracle when you needed one?

The doorbell interrupted the awkward moment.

Apparently, miracles still happened.

"I'll get it!" I practically shouted as I jumped out of my seat, shoving Rafa down as he attempted to stand as well.

I raced to the door, yanked it open, and was relieved as fuck when I saw my brother and best friend, Onyx, standing on the porch. He wasn't my brother by blood, we belonged to the same motorcycle club, the Hounds of Hellfire.

Although it wasn't until we were adults, we'd met through Bridget since his dad was the much younger brother of her father, Pierce. Making my "family" tree even more convoluted, Pierce had once been the president of my MC and married to my dad's sister, Laina...which was how I was related to Bridget.

It was confusing as fuck to anyone who wasn't Italian. Or in the family. Even I struggled to keep it all straight sometimes.

Bridget encouraged me to focus on art in college and then suggested that I think about tattooing. I'd worked at a small shop in Atlanta for a while, then landed an apprenticeship with a highly prestigious tattoo studio in Atlanta.

Onyx worked at Silver Ink, the tattoo shop owned by the Silver Saints, when Mac and Bridget introduced us. The manager, Patriot, offered me a job, but I hesitated to take it. I'd grown up around the Saints. Hell, Mac had been the one to teach me to ride. I didn't want anything I hadn't earned, but when Patriot, the manager of the studio, saw my work, he talked me into it. Onyx and I grew as close as brothers, so when he decided to prospect with the Hounds of Hellfire, I was happy for him. Even though it meant they stole him away to work at their studio out in Riverstone.

Eventually, though, Onyx convinced me to do the same. It turned out to be one of the best decisions I'd ever made.

"Yo," he greeted. "Bridget mentioned *Mamma* Emilia was cookin'."

Sunday dinners at any DeLuca house were a "more the merrier" situation, so after experiencing some of my *mamma's*—or Aunt Giulia's—cooking, some of my MC brothers were known to drop by from time to time. The few who knew who I really was.

"Fair warning, the *mammas* are on about marriage and babies again."

Onyx blanched and stepped backward, but I grabbed his cut and dragged him into the house. "Didn't mean you could leave, *fratello*," I grunted. Then I raised my voice as I shoved him into the dining room. "Heyyy, look who we have here!"

"Reeve!" my mother exclaimed, jumping to her feet and running over to hug him. She was one of the only people who ever got away with calling him by his real name.

"What about you, *cucciolo*?" she asked when she let him go. "Have you found a girl to give me more grandbabies?"

"Ahhh, no," Onyx replied uneasily.

She reached up and whacked him on the back of the head, the same as she would any boy she considered to be like a son. "What is it with you boys? Too busy with work or running around like fools to find a good woman and make babies."

"Now, now, Emilia," Fonso piped up, his face serious, but his eyes dancing with laughter. "I'm sure they get plenty of practice."

My *mamma* gasped and made the sign of the cross.

I nearly rolled my eyes. It had been a long time since I'd been interested in a relationship, and I'd never been a fling kind of guy.

Besides, if any of my single brothers or I tried to bring a one-night stand or "club bunny" to the clubhouse, King—our prez—would have our asses. He'd never liked it, but he'd made it an iron-clad rule once he got married and had a kid.

"Blaze and Courtney will be having their baby in

three months," Onyx offered, referring to our VP and his old lady.

"Hmm," *Mamma* sniffed. "Well, at least some of those Hounds are doing right by their mothers."

"Don't worry, *Mamma*," my sister said sweetly. "I'll give you a whole houseful of grandbabies."

I frowned at sixteen-year-old Elena, matching the expression of her twin, Gavin. Her father didn't look any happier.

"Just how are you gonna do that?" I growled.

Her eyes narrowed, and she shot a withering stare at each of us before she snapped, "You can't keep all the boys away from me forever, Matteo."

I snorted. "Bullshit."

"Watch me," growled Gavin.

Fonso just nodded his head in solidarity. That was the most we were gonna get from him. He let her brothers do the dirty work so he wouldn't have to be the bag guy with his princess. We'd all been wrapped around Elena's finger since the day she was born, so I didn't hold a grudge against him for wanting to stay on the pedestal she'd put him on.

"Language!" Aunt Giulia scolded, slapping me upside the back of the head since she'd been walking past me when I cursed.

"Ouch, *Zia*!" I grunted, rubbing the sore spot.

She glared at me, then smiled warmly at Onyx. "Let me get you a plate."

He smiled gratefully and followed her over to the spread of food on the massive kitchen island.

When my mother didn't start in on me again, I warily returned to my seat at the table to finish my meal.

"Ink."

I turned my head to look at Domenico De Angelis, a member of the family who worked for Rafa here in Georgia.

"We could use your help with a"—he paused and glanced around for a second—"situation this week. There might be a connection to the Hounds."

I shook my head. "Gotta talk to King." Anything involving the MC needed to be discussed with my prez before anyone else.

"It's family business," Domenico said with a frown.

"Not if it involves the Hounds of Hellfire," Rafa chimed in, backing me up. "Besides, King isn't likely to let us borrow Ink anytime soon anyway."

"Why not?" asked Marco, one of Rafa's brothers.

"Don't know," I drawled sarcastically, leaning back in my chair. "Maybe 'cause last time you got me shot?"

1

ANNIKA

"Are you on the way to Hellbound Studio?" Rachel asked, her voice playing through my Jeep's speaker.

My ride was adorable...and also the last present I got from my mom and dad. So even though most of my friends had gotten new cars for our high school graduation, I hadn't been the slightest bit envious. I planned to drive this baby until the wheels fell off.

"I am," I confirmed with a wide grin that she couldn't see.

"I'm so bummed that I couldn't be there with you for this. Although it's probably for the best because I doubt I would've been able to walk out of the tattoo parlor without any ink of my own, and we both know how that would've gone down with my parents."

I laughed, picturing the hissy fit her mom would have pitched at the sight of a tattoo on her daughter's unblemished skin. Something she wouldn't have been able to hide during their annual trip to the Bahamas, which was where she was this week. "Forget heading off to college in a couple of weeks. You would have been locked in your room for the next year."

She snorted. "Let's be real. It would be at least two years."

"Probably," I agreed. "Remind me not to go swimming at your house if your parents are around. She might decide I'm a bad influence and not let us hang out together anymore."

"Like I would ever let that happen. I might not put my foot down with my parents very often, but if they went after my bestie, you best believe they'd have a fight on their hands."

I knew she meant every word of her vow, and hearing how much I meant to her made me sniffle. "Cut it out, or I'm going to be crying before they even start the tattoo."

"Maybe there will be a hot guy to hold your hand

during the whole thing since I'm not there to do it," she teased.

I rolled my eyes. "Not gonna happen. This isn't one of the romcoms we love to watch on our movie nights."

"But it could be."

My best friend was much more optimistic than I was. Losing my parents a couple of years ago made me see the world differently. I wasn't as carefree as I used to be.

"I'm almost there," I told her as I turned onto the road where the tattoo parlor was located.

"Then I guess I'll let you go." Her laughter drifted through the line. "Which is probably for the best because my mom will come looking for me any minute. We're going snorkeling today."

"Sounds as though you're going to have lots of fun. Tell your mom and dad I said hello."

"Will do." Knowing my bestie how I did, I wasn't surprised when she added, "The water here is awesome, but I hope you have way more fun than me. With a sexy tattoo artist who pops your cherry so you don't have to worry about being the only virgin on campus."

"You're ridiculous." I turned into the parking lot, shaking my head.

"And that's why you love me," she quipped.

"Only because I didn't know better when we became best friends," I teased, pulling into a parking spot. "Good luck finding a hottie who'll help you out with the same potential problem I'll have when I get to college since you've never slept with anyone either."

"I wish," she muttered. "But we both know my mom would literally throw herself between any interesting guy and me to make sure nothing happens."

"For real."

We shared a laugh over the mental image of her mom shoving between Rachel and some random man on the beach before hanging up. Then I hopped out of my Jeep.

I was nervous as I walked into Hellbound Studio, but that didn't stop me from going inside. I'd wanted a tattoo for two years, but since I only turned eighteen last month, I hadn't been able to get one until then. My birthday was so close to my parents' anniversary, so I decided just to wait and have it done today since that would bring extra meaning to the tattoo.

My nerves combined with the summer heat, making my palms sweaty as I crossed the parking lot.

I rubbed them against my shorts before taking a deep breath. Then I yanked the door open and strode inside, trying to look more confident than I felt when the guy behind the counter looked up and flashed me a grin.

He didn't look much older than me, but he had several tattoos on his left arm, so he fit with the place. "Hey, how can I help you?"

"I have an appointment with Onyx."

He tapped on the keyboard, then asked, "Annika Lee?"

I nodded. "Yup."

"And this is your first tattoo?"

Another nod. "Yeah."

He scanned this information. "Looks like you already filled out all the paperwork online, so I just need to see your driver's license."

I grabbed my wallet from my purse and tugged out my identification. Sliding it across the counter, I murmured, "Here you go."

He scanned my license into their system before handing it back to me. "Now you're all set for when Onyx is ready to take you back. Should be any minute now."

"Great."

Faster was definitely better, as far as I was

concerned. Although I'd been looking forward to this day for so long, I didn't trust myself not to chicken out before my appointment even got started.

As he answered the ringing phone, I wandered over to the waiting area. When I searched online for a tattoo shop, Hellbound Studio had been rated the best in Georgia, not just in my little town of Riverstone. It was on Main Street, across from The Fuel & Flame Diner, but I had never been to either business since the local motorcycle club owned them. The fit my uncle would pitch if he ever learned I came here would rival Rachel's mom's if she'd been with me.

Hellbound Studio wasn't anything like I'd pictured in my head. The cinder block walls were painted white, and the floor was decorative concrete with a dark and light gray pattern. The wood beams in the ceiling were exposed, and so was the ductwork, giving the place an industrial feel. But the lighting was bright, and there wasn't a speck of dust that I could see.

Instead of sitting down, I studied the framed pictures on the wall. They were sketches of what I assumed were tattoos that the Hellbound artists had done, and they were all impressive. "Annika?"

Turning, I smile at the man standing in front of the reception counter. "That's me. You're Onyx?"

"Yup," he confirmed with a lift of his chin. "From the note when you booked your appointment, it sounded like you know exactly what you want. Did you bring any photos or drawings that I can use as a reference?"

Crossing to him, I pulled my phone from my purse to show him what I found online, pointing out the flowers first. "I was hoping you could do a heritage rose like this one."

"I can draw that."

Then I swiped to a photo of a heart-shaped pocket watch with Roman numerals on the face. "And I want the hands to point to eight and eleven."

"Today's date? It has special meaning for you?" he asked as he scrolled through the images I saved in a folder on my phone.

I swallowed the lump in my throat that was always there when I talked about my mom and dad. "It's when my parents got married. I thought it would be a good way to honor them and how much they loved each other."

"Loved?"

"Yeah, I lost them two years ago."

I didn't give him any additional details because I'd never make it through this appointment if I did.

Talking about their deaths was too hard for me, even after this much time had passed.

"I get it." Onyx lifted his shirt and twisted to the side to show me the black ink on his back. "Had this done to honor my mom. Lost her when I was a teenager. It's what got me interested in becoming a tattoo artist."

I hadn't expected the tall, muscular, tattooed biker to open up to me like that, but I felt much more at ease with his confession. "I hate that you had to go through a loss like that, but I'm glad you understand why I want this particular tattoo. It makes me feel a little more comfortable with you being the one to draw it."

He dropped his shirt back into place and leaned his hip against the reception counter. "You have nothing to worry about. I'm the best in the business."

"Most of Ink's clients would disagree," the guy behind the counter murmured.

"Ignore Jay. He's a prospect who just started answering the phones for us last week. He has no fucking clue what he's talking about." Crossing his arms over his chest, Onyx smiled at me. "For the clock face, you want the short hand on eight and the long one on eleven?"

"That's exactly what I want."

2

INK

I carefully placed a bandage over the fresh tattoo I'd just inked onto my cousin's rib cage.

"You know how to take care of it, *fratello*?" I asked, not really paying attention and pretty much on autopilot.

Marcello rolled his eyes as he curled his abs up into a sitting position. "No, after thirteen tattoos, I forgot. You wanna enlighten me?"

I tossed him a dirty look and grunted, *"Cazzo zito, stronzo."*

He grinned and hopped off the table I used when the piece's location required my client to lie down.

Shoving my rolling chair toward a small station

that held my cleaning supplies, my mind was already on my next appointment.

I loved my job, and at the core, my art was a connection to my father. Although he had many responsibilities for The Family, he always found time for me and his art. He'd taught me everything he knew.

He'd loved my mom and me fiercely, and inside our home, it was easy to pretend we were a typical family. But I was a DeLuca, and that changed everything when I walked outside the door.

Just like Gabbi had said, when people heard the name DeLuca, it put the fear of God into them.

Why?

Because they were the fucking Mafia.

It had taken a toll on my mom, so when my father was murdered, she'd had enough. I was ten and didn't understand why she was taking me away from my life and family, moving us from New York City to Georgia.

My mom had been close to my dad's sister, Laina. Even after the family had pretty much disowned her for running off with the president of a questionable motorcycle club. They'd been really old school in those days. Which would have been a huge fucking problem for me since I'd chosen a life outside The Family. Thankfully, the younger generations were more open-minded.

The coincidental thing about the whole situation was that Laina and my dad's brother, Salvatore, had moved to Georgia to take over the Southern branches before he married Giulia. Despite being only a half hour from each other at the most, their families didn't even speak.

However, Salvatore had brought his wife and kids to New York frequently, so they were the only people who were familiar to me. They were family.

My mom didn't want me to have anything to do with The Family, so she wasn't happy that I spent a lot of time with my DeLuca cousins.

I was close with Laina's family too, though, and as I got older, I knew I didn't want to be a part of the Mafia. Although I remained close to my family, I distanced myself from the darker side of their life. Sal tried to change my mind, but he didn't push too hard. Then he went to prison, and Rafa took over as underboss. He fully supported my choice and didn't even try to convince me to work for him. Not that I didn't get pulled into Family shit from time to time.

I'd spent more and more time with the Silver

Saints, and by the time I was an adult, I saw the "family" I needed in a motorcycle club. I was related to the DeLucas by blood, and that carried a fuck ton of weight to Italians, especially in The Family. But the members of the Silver Saints were just as tightly bound. Even more so in some ways.

They weren't a brotherhood by blood, but their loyalty to the club and each other was stronger than shared DNA because it was a choice. It was earned. It was a pledge.

Mac tried to talk me into becoming a prospect for the Silver Saints, but I didn't want to patch into a club where I'd never know if I'd truly earned my place.

The same went for the Iron Rogues MC. Fox, their prez, was tight with my cousin Nic—the head of The Family. I'd always worry that he had secured my cut for me.

Then Onyx convinced me to consider coming to work at Hellbound Studio, making a pitch for prospecting with the Hounds in the process. I hadn't immediately rejected the idea because, in a roundabout way, there was still a connection to the DeLucas. However, the ties were far enough apart that I could fly under the radar while still having Nic's approval.

Of course, having a tech genius like Wizard patched meant my background came out the second I applied to be a prospect. But while a few of the officers knew about my familial ties, they'd allowed me to keep it mostly to myself.

But seeing as the two groups seemed to be constantly crossing paths and using each other's resources, being Matteo "Ink" Donovan—I'd used my middle name as my surname when I applied—had quickly run its course.

The difference with the Hounds is that they didn't give a fuck who my blood relations were. I was just Ink. A Hounds of Hellfire brother, enforcer, and tattoo artist.

When I came to work at Hellbound Studio with Onyx, my client list quickly filled up. My waiting list was cut off at six months, so I packed some of my days with appointments in order to have lighter ones.

Today was back-to-back, so I left Marco to see himself out. But as I swiveled back toward the table, a voice floated to my ears, making me freeze.

It was sweet while being just husky enough to make it incredibly sexy.

My feet seemed to have a mind of their own, and when I stood, they walked me straight toward the front of the studio.

Onyx was lazily leaning a hip on the reception counter with his arms crossed and a smile on his face.

I understood his disarming demeanor when my eyes landed on the woman he was talking to.

Holy shit.

Her long dark blond hair was in a loose braid, hanging down her back with flyaway strands framing her heart-shaped face. Her blue eyes were so light, they almost looked like ice. Surrounded by lashes that matched the color of her hair. Her creamy skin was pale, emphasizing the natural pink bloom on her high cheekbones.

A sensual quality to her plump lips made me want to bite them before ravishing them. As my gaze continued down, my body came roaring to life with a vengeance. I couldn't remember the last time I'd been interested in a woman, and all of a sudden, I was practically sweating from the hunger and need coursing through me.

Damn, she was sexy as fuck. She looked soft all over, making me ache to feel her sweet, curvy body pressed against my hard one.

She had big, luscious tits, deliciously thick thighs, and wide, round hips that were perfect for holding while I slammed into her from behind. And for having babies. *Whoa! Where the fuck had that thought come from?*

The shock wore off quickly, and I knew deep down in my soul that this woman was meant to be mine.

When my gaze returned to her face, I zeroed in on her soft expression. There was a sadness lurking in there that made me want to protect her and fix whatever was causing her pain.

"That's why I chose a pocket watch. I do something to remember them every August for their anniversary, but I want to have them with me all the time," she told Onyx softly.

My brow furrowed at her words. Was she here for a tattoo?

The bell on the door jangled, but all of my focus was on my woman.

"Hey, Ink," my next client greeted.

I lifted my chin in his direction but kept my gaze on her.

"I want it on my upper thigh."

I was moving before I even realized it. "Onyx is gonna do your tattoo this time, Neil," I called out.

Both Onyx and the woman turned their heads to look at me when I approached.

"I'll be doing your ink, baby," I grunted.

Onyx's expression was confused until his gaze bounced back and forth between me and my girl. "Uh, Annika, this is Ink. Guess there's been a change. Seems I've been double booked. Ink's the best there is. He'll take care of you."

Annika—fucking beautiful name—double blinked, her ice-blue eyes wide as she stared at me. I wanted to smile at the heat sparking in them, especially since I could tell she was taken aback by it.

She didn't know me yet, so I suppressed the laugh and smiled instead.

"C'mon, *dolcezza*," I murmured, putting my hand at the small of her back and guiding her toward my booth. When we reached it, I gestured for her to sit in the chair and popped down onto my stool and rolled next to her.

"Tell me about the tattoo," I requested, staring boldly into her clear, blue orbs.

Her voice was soft as she explained about her parents and what she'd chosen to have inked on her skin in remembrance. It was clear that she missed them and had loved and been loved in return. Her idea was beautiful, and I couldn't wait to start sketching her design.

When she finished, I gave her a soft smile and

held out my left arm, showing her the underside and pointed to a spot near the crease of my elbow. There was a dripping paint palette and brush. If you looked close enough, the bristles formed an outline of a father holding the hand on his young son as they walked away. "Had that done for my dad when I was fifteen."

Annika stared at the art for a moment, then raised her eyes up to meet mine. They sparkled with unshed tears, and she placed her hand on my wrist, giving it a gentle squeeze. "I'm sorry, Ink."

"Me too, *dolcezza*," I replied. Then I cocked my head to the side and heat filled my gaze, bringing a pretty blush to her cheeks. "Matteo. Call me Matteo, baby."

"Okay," she whispered, a pretty smile lighting up her beautiful face. When she released my wrist, it felt like a bolt of electricity arced between us, sizzling over my skin and shooting straight to my dick.

My pants were suddenly way too fucking tight, so I inhaled deeply and swiveled my stool just slightly to hide my reaction. I reached for a pad and pencil, ready to get started, but her phone rang.

"Oops. Sorry," she apologized, pink rushing to her cheeks. The corners of her lips dropped into a confused frown when she checked the caller ID. "It's my school. I'm so sorry, but I just want to make sure everything is okay."

"Whatever you need, *dolcezza*," I told her with a nonchalant wave. "Gonna get shit ready."

She smiled and hit the accept button before raising the phone to her ear. "Hello? Yes, I'm Annika Lee."

The other person started talking, but I couldn't hear their side of the conversation. I took the opportunity to study my girl a little more, but I didn't get much of a chance before she gasped and went rigid. "What do you mean it bounced?"

They said something, and she shook her head. "That's impossible. Did you call the bank to verify the check?"

She listened again, all color draining from her face. "I'll...um...I'll get back to you. Um, how long do I have before you won't hold my classes?" Her eyes closed, and her head drooped forward. "Okay. Thank you," she whispered, her voice steeped in despair and confusion.

When she hung up, she sat in silence for a minute, her eyes glued to her phone.

"What's going on, Annika?"

Her head lifted and swiveled so that our gazes

collided. "I...um...I paid my tuition for college in the fall, and...it didn't go through. I don't–I don't understand. The money is there. I don't know what's happening."

"Relax, *dolcezza*," I murmured. "I can help. We'll figure this out."

3

ANNIKA

Matteo was sexier than any man deserved to be. Even after the shock I'd gotten during that phone call, I was having a hard time ignoring my attraction to him. Which I had a feeling most women would understand because of how hot he was.

He was tall with lean muscles and a butt that looked great in his jeans. His short hair was inky black and matched the chinstrap beard on his brutally masculine face. His bright-blue eyes had an intensity that made me want to squirm...but in a good way.

With the black tattoos on both of his arms and the leather vest that announced to the world that he was a member of the Hounds of Hellfire, there was no denying Matteo had a dangerous vibe. But he was a tattoo artist, not a lawyer or banker.

His offer was kind, but it didn't make any more sense than what I'd just been told by the person from my college's business office.

"How can you help? This has to be a glitch at the bank. There was no reason for my check to have bounced."

I didn't like talking about how much my parents had left me when they died. I would've gladly given it all back to just have a little more time with them, but they had ensured that I had more than enough to do anything I wanted with my life. If I wanted to skip college and tour the world, I could travel until I was old and gray...and there would still be money left for my retirement. Between my dad's investments, my childhood home, and their rather large life insurance policies, I had more money than I knew what to do with.

"Do you use your bank's app?"

"Yeah, but that's not going to help solve this problem because my trust doesn't show up there. Only my personal account, and the check for my tuition wasn't written on it," I explained, my brows drawing together. "It's never been an issue before because my uncle just transferred over whatever I needed."

Matteo crossed his arms over his chest, drawing my attention to the full tattoo sleeves on both of them. "Your uncle?"

My words came out in a rush as I tried to come up with a reason for the mix-up at the bank. "I only turned eighteen last month, so he handled everything for me as my guardian until now. The investment accounts, checking...everything related to the trust. He said it was gonna take a little while for all of the paperwork to transfer everything into my name, but I didn't think there would be an issue with me writing a check for tuition since it was specified in my trust, and I'm listed on the account. Maybe it's just because of the amount, and he still needs to sign off on it."

"Could be," he conceded, sounding unconvinced.

I shook my head. "No, that can't be right because the woman from the college said it came back as insufficient funds."

"Only one reason that happens, and it sounds like there's only one person who can be responsible for it if your uncle has been managing the trust for you until you were old enough to take care of it yourself."

My stomach was in knots. "My dad arranged all the details in his will. Down to Uncle Alec moving into our house so that I didn't have to be uprooted in the middle of high school."

"I hate to break it to you, *dolcezza*, but it shouldn't take the bank an entire month to move shit into your name." He interlaced our fingers and gave my hand a comforting squeeze.

"You think my uncle lied to me?" I asked.

He heaved a deep sigh and nodded. "Yeah, and if the money isn't in that account, that's probably why he's been slow with the paperwork. Odds are good that he wanted to hide it from you as long as he could."

My shoulders slumped, and I buried my face in my hands. "I can't believe this is happening."

"Are you and your uncle close?"

Glancing up at Matteo, I grimaced. "Not really. I always assumed he was awkward with me because he didn't know what to do with a teenage girl, but maybe it was because he's been robbing me blind this entire time."

He wrapped his arms around me and pulled me against his chest. "We're gonna find out what happened. No matter what your uncle pulled, you're going to be okay."

My voice was muffled as I mumbled, "Don't make promises you can't possibly keep. If Uncle Alec did what I'm starting to suspect, I will need a lawyer. And an accountant to see how much damage he did."

He leaned back and pressed a finger under my chin. When our gazes met, he flashed me a cocky smirk. "Then I guess it's a good thing I have a lawyer on speed dial."

"You do?" I squeaked, wondering why a tattoo artist would need the services of an attorney so often.

Matteo chuckled. "Not for whatever reason just popped into your pretty little head. Ash is one of my club brothers."

"Sorry." I flashed him an apologetic smile.

"It's okay, *dolcezza*. I understand why you'd be suspicious of everyone right now."

"Maybe I'm jumping the gun, and this really all was a glitch."

Instead of arguing with me, he jerked his chin toward my phone. "Call the bank and see what they say."

Pulling up the nearest branch in my map app, I clicked on their phone number and waited for someone to answer. "Riverstone Bank, how may I help you?"

"Hello, this is Annika Lee. Could you look up a transaction for me and let me know why it didn't clear?"

"Certainly, I'll just need some information from you to verify your identity first."

Glancing up at Matteo, I whispered, "Can you give me a second? She won't tell me anything until I prove who I am."

"Sure."

After he stepped out of the tattoo booth, I gave her my birthdate, social security number, and address. Then she replied, "Okay, I'm pulling up the account now. Is this the check for $16,000 that we declined a few days ago?"

I opened the door so Matteo knew it was okay to come back inside. He gave a pointed look at the phone, so I put it in speaker mode as I said, "Yes, made payable to Cornerstone College."

"I can confirm that it was rejected due to insufficient funds. You or the trustee listed on the account will need to deposit additional funds before we can approve this transaction."

"I don't understand. There should have been plenty of money in that account since there's an annual disbursement from the trust's investment portfolio on my birthday, which was only last month."

"There would have been, except for the withdrawal of $50,000 last week."

Her answer left me speechless. I knew that the bulk of my inheritance was in my brokerage account and the house—which I owned outright—but there was no reason for my uncle to have drawn down the balance on the trust's checking account. And there was no reason for him to have pulled out that much money.

Matteo took the phone from my trembling fingers and demanded, "Print out statements for the past two years and have them waiting for Miss Lee. Someone will come in to pick them up for her today."

He didn't give the banker the chance to argue, jabbing his finger against the screen to end the call.

"We're gonna get to the bottom of this," he promised, grabbing his phone from the counter behind him.

I couldn't hear what the other person said, but I assumed it was the guy he'd mentioned when he said, "Sorry to interrupt the festivities, but my girl needs a lawyer. You gotta come back on the earliest flight you can find."

I was confused as to why he was calling me his girl but also impressed by the lengths his club brother would go to for him when he disconnected the call a moment later and said, "Ash will be here tomorrow at the latest. He and his new wife need to fly in from Vegas."

"New wife?" I echoed, hoping he meant they got married sometime this year and were just enjoying a fun getaway together.

"Yeah, he got tired of dealing with his mother-in-law, so he and Nora eloped to Vegas without telling anyone." He shook his head with a deep laugh. "I'm sure there's gonna be hell to pay with her for that decision."

My eyes widened. "And you're making him come back early to face her?"

"Not making him do shit." Tugging me to my feet, Matteo shrugged. "He could've told me to wait, but his nosy ass probably wants to get a look at you."

"Me?" I asked, pointing at my chest.

"Who else would it be when I've never called anyone 'my girl' before you?"

"Yeah, I was kinda wondering about that part

since we literally just met, but then you threw me with the fact that you called your friend during his elopement to tell him to come back and help me...and he's doing it." I blinked up at him, wondering how so many things could change in such a short amount of time. "I really don't understand what's happening right now."

"That's easy, *dolcezza*. I'm gonna take you to the compound to see another brother who can help figure out the banking shit while we wait for Ash to come back from Vegas."

Although the situation with my uncle was awful, Rachel was going to have a field day over the fact that she'd been right about a sexy tattoo artist helping me—just through something a heck of a little bigger than the pain from being inked.

4

INK

I wasn't about to let Annika out of my sight until I'd made it clear to the world that she belonged to me. And I was itching to feel her curves wrapped around me as we flew into the wind on my motorcycle. I'd never let a woman on my bike, not even family, so I was a little surprised that I hadn't even hesitated when deciding how we'd get to the compound.

"Give me your keys, *dolcezza*," I ordered, holding out one hand while the other kept a firm grip on hers. "Onyx or a prospect will bring your car to the clubhouse."

Annika blinked up at me, then excitement brightened her eyes. "Are we going to take your motorcycle?"

"You like that idea?" I asked with a lazy smile. "Taking a ride with me?"

A deep blush colored Annika's cheeks, but she nodded. "I've never ridden on a motorcycle."

"You'll only ever ride on one, baby," I said in a low voice that made her shiver. I fucking loved when she did that. It was sexy as hell.

She bit her lip as she pulled her keys from her purse and handed them to me. Then she offered no resistance as I guided her up to the front and tossed them to Jay. "Cancel my appointments for the rest of the week. And get Annika's car back to the compound." I glared at him pointedly and growled, "One scratch, and you'll be out on your ass, probie."

He jerked his chin up and down quickly. "Done."

My bike was parked in a gated lot behind the shop, so I took Annika to the back door and out into the sunshine. It was a perfect day to ride. If we hadn't been in the middle of dealing with her uncle's shit, I'd have put off going to the clubhouse and taken her out for a few hours. As soon as it was handled, I was gonna take her for a long ride. In more ways than one.

When we were standing beside my hog, I

retrieved a helmet from one of the saddle bags and gently popped it onto Annika's head.

"Cute as fuck," I murmured with a smirk and a slight shake of my head. Then I shrugged off my cut and helped her into it as well. I looked her over and frowned. While she looked amazing in my clothes, I didn't like that her arms and legs would be so exposed on the road. I'd have to be extra cautious until I could get her a set of leathers and her own helmet.

"Wait here, *dolcezza*," I ordered. Jogging over to the gate, I dug my keys out of my pocket, then unlocked it and opened the big door. Then I returned for my bike, and we walked out of the small lot before I closed and locked the gate again. Returning to her side, I swung my leg over the seat and got settled before instructing her on how to climb behind me. Once I knew that she was good back there, I fired up the engine.

When we were ready to go, I glanced back at my girl. "Hold on tight, *dolcezza*."

As I suspected, the ride was too fucking short. Annika felt amazing wrapped around me and since we'd just met, it was the only way I'd be between those thighs right now.

King was waiting for me when I drove into the compound and parked in front of the clubhouse.

I shouldn't have been surprised. Everything involving the club had to be run by the president first. His authority on club matters was absolute, and he kept a tight rein on it all. To some, it might have been seen as micromanaging, but we knew that even though King controlled every aspect of club business, he did it to make sure shit got done and that it happened in a way that screwups wouldn't damage the club.

Besides, he rewarded our loyalty with his trust in the right circumstances. He knew when someone needed autonomy and gave them the freedom to accomplish their goal without interference.

And no matter who was at fault for anything that happened, he took responsibility for our failures while attributing any successes to the whole club.

After helping Annika off the bike and dismounting, I grabbed her hand and met him at the door.

"Ash or Onyx?" I questioned wryly. Sometimes my brothers gossiped like teenage girls.

King's scowl—his permanent expression, for the most part—stayed firmly in place, but amusement glinted in his eyes. "Both," he answered before his gaze shifted to Annika, briefly lingering on my cut. "This her?"

"Yeah."

He observed her thoughtfully for a second, then lifted his chin in greeting. "I'm King, president of the Hounds of Hellfire. You're welcome here, and no one will hurt you. Suggest you keep that cut on, though. Don't need Ink killin' anybody."

Annika giggled, but it trailed off when King's face remained serious. Obviously confused, she glanced up at me. Doubting that she was ready for that much truth, I didn't comment, just tugged her hand and headed inside.

Upon entering, I turned her in the opposite direction of a hallway that led to offices and took her into the lounge instead.

The room definitely had a typical biker vibe.

The giant recreation area had black leather couches along the walls, a pool table in the middle, and several big-screen televisions. Across from it was a bar lined with stools that had black leather saddle seats and chrome legs. The wall behind it was stocked with liquor nearly from the floor to the ceiling. And a few other drinks, mostly for the old ladies. Especially nonalcoholic options because my brothers knocked their women up as fast as possible.

Couldn't say I didn't understand anymore. I wanted Annika bound to me in every way—property patch, ring, and a swollen belly.

King's wife, Stella, sat at the bar with an e-reader in one hand while she used the other to rock a baby carrier holding their four-month-old son, Cadell. Their dog, Cerberus, was perched on the floor beside her, his eyes glued to the baby. The muscular giant, a Cane Corso who looked as deadly as he was trained to be, had shocked the fuck out of all of us when he turned into some kind of doggy "manny," rarely leaving Cadell's side since he'd been born.

Although he'd loosened up lately and gone back to putting the fear of hell—hence being named after the three-headed dog guarding the underworld—into strangers. Unless he didn't consider them a threat, then he just ignored their existence altogether.

Most people shied away from him, put off by his fearsome presence and cold attitude. What they didn't know—and neither had I before I met him—was that, like most of his breed, he was extremely affectionate with anyone he grew attached to. I'd been shocked as fuck the first time I saw him cuddling with one of my brothers. After I scooped my jaw up off the ground, King told me that was how

Cerberus showed approval and love. He recognized that we shared his loyalty to the prez.

He'd also quickly figured out which of us were the biggest suckers and shamelessly begged for attention when we were near. Including me. Scariest fucking dog I'd ever seen, and I couldn't resist when he flopped on his back in front of me, demanding I rub his belly.

His head lifted when King stalked across the room, but he didn't pay them any more attention when King turned Stella's stool around to face him, then wrapped his arms around her and kissed her like he hadn't seen her in a year.

"Hey, baby," he greeted her softly when they parted.

I glanced down at Annika and nearly laughed at the stunned expression on her face as she watched the couple.

When I shifted my gaze back toward King and Stella, I frowned, noticing Cerberus was no longer sitting near them. My gaze darted around, worried that he would scare the shit out of Annika, but I didn't see him.

"Hello. Aren't you just adorable?"

Annika's sweet tone drew my attention as she bent forward and giggled.

I rolled my eyes when I saw the shameless pet rubbing his head against her legs, wagging his tail, and staring up at her with big, puppy dog eyes that a badass dog like him should not have been able to pull off.

She scratched him under the chin and giggled when his tongue lolled out the side of his mouth.

"Now who's the sucker?" I muttered at Cerberus. Not that I didn't understand his desire for Annika's affection. In fact, I was fucking horrified to realize that I was a little jealous. Of a damn dog.

"Who is this?" she asked affectionately.

I kind of hated him right at that moment.

"He used to be a badass guard dog," I drawled. "Not sure what to call this thing."

"Cerberus," King answered in an exasperated tone.

"The three-headed dog that guards hell," I explained as if I was insulting the beast for being named after a mythical monster.

Cerberus turned his head to stare up at me, and I could practically hear him gloating when Annika scratched him again.

Shaking my head to clear away my ridiculous thoughts, I refocused on Annika's current situation.

Echo—our Road Captain—was lounging on one

of the sofas, a beer in one hand and his other arm curled around his old lady, Violet. They'd been talking quietly with Ace—our treasurer and money manager with the Midas touch—and two other enforcers, Cruze and Fallon, when we entered the room.

They went silent now, looking in our direction. All eyes went to my cut before landing on me, the question clear in their expressions. I nodded, and while Cruze and Fallon grunted and rolled their eyes, Ace, Echo, and Violet grinned. Stella clapped her hands excitedly, then gasped and checked the baby carrier before sighing in relief, making King chuckle.

"Need you two to meet me in Wizard's office," I told Ace and Echo. "Club shit."

"Blaze is on his way," King added.

I lifted my chin in acknowledgment, then pivoted, ignoring Cerberus's offended growl when I dragged Annika away. We strode down the hallway that led to the offices and other rooms. Like an armory. An interrogation cell. And a SCIF, also known as a skiff room. It was a secure room or data center that guarded sensitive security information from surveillance and leaks.

That level of privacy was necessary in the clubhouse when it came to the kinds of businesses and activities the Hounds of Hellfire were involved in. Particularly when it came to...*bending* the letter of the law.

The Hounds had just as fearsome of a reputation as the most violent and lethal clubs out there. But we lived by a code, one that was honorable, loyal, and fair. We did plenty of illegal shit, and people who needed killing didn't usually last long on our radar. We had our own brand of justice, and when the laws of the land didn't get the job done, we ventured into some dark gray areas.

We also had legitimate businesses, like Hellbound Studio, as well as a bar, diner, garage, and a few others. And Ace's mad skills in the stock market kept the club finances well in the black.

However, our main source of income wasn't something we advertised.

When we reached a closed door that had a fingerprint and retinal scanner, I hit a fat red button just below them.

"A doorbell?" Annika guessed, studying the button that was straight out of a superhero comic.

"Sort of. Wizard is our tech guy. He deals with a lot of sensitive shit. Not a good idea for visitors or prospects to accidentally walk in. Only Wizard,

King, and our VP, Blaze, have access through the scanners. And he wears headphones a lot. You push that, it sends a signal to his headphones. Plays a tone that lets him know someone is here or needs something."

She nodded and murmured, "Smart. But, um…"

"Why the big red button?"

Annika nodded, a smile playing at the corners of her mouth.

"Because Blaze has a warped sense of humor and thought it was hilarious," I explained. "Never push the big red button."

She burst into laughter just as the door buzzed, and I was able to turn the handle and usher her inside. When she saw the interior of the room, her eyes went wide, and her mouth formed a little O.

It was pretty impressive, with a wall of monitors and more computers on the desk, along with random gadgets—some of which were probably classified—all around the room.

Wizard was typing on a laptop, frowning intensely at the screen and muttering to himself. "Gonna kick someone's ass if they don't quit messing with this shit," he grumbled as he leaned back in his chair. He whipped his reading glasses off his face and tossed them onto the desk. "Or better yet, gonna cut off each finger before I put a bull..." He trailed off when he finally swiveled his chair in our direction and spotted Annika.

Why was all the bloodthirsty shit coming out of their mouths in front of her? They were gonna send my woman running before I had the chance to slowly introduce her to the reality of life with a motorcycle club.

"Hey, there," he greeted, his scowl morphing into a lopsided smile while he absently hit something on the keyboard that made his screen go black. "Video games are so violent these days."

Annika shrugged. "I've never played one."

Wizard's eyes bulged, and his mouth opened and closed several times.

"Making Wizard speechless. Impressive, *dolcezza*."

"Never?" he eventually asked.

"Nope."

"Well, shit. You need schooling, *dolcezza*." He grinned at me when he called her sweetness in Italian.

"Keep it up," I growled. "See what happens."

"I'm not afraid of concrete shoes," Wizard quipped.

I raised my brow. "Give me more credit than

that, brother. Getting rid of a body has evolved with so much creativity."

Wizard opened his mouth but was cut off by King's arrival. "Shut the fuck up, Wizard," he growled. "I'll give Ink more than credit for the fact that you're still breathing. Pull shit like that with Stella, and I'd be using you as target practice."

"Where is Thea, anyway?" Echo mused as he sauntered in behind Blaze and Ace. "I'm sure she'd like to see you flirting with Ink's woman. Inspiration for her novels."

Wizard's expression darkened, and his hands balled into fists. "Point taken, assholes."

Ace rolled his eyes and strolled over to the couch on the wall opposite Wizard's desk. "Might want to watch your words around company," he muttered as he sat down.

Shit.

I was almost afraid to look down at Annika, but when I did, I was surprised to see her watching us with humor rather than horror.

"Just out of curiosity. Are you guys serious or blowing smoke?" she asked suddenly.

"Would option one freak you out?" I queried in return.

She thought for a minute, then shrugged. "I

guess not. I mean, it's not as though I didn't have some idea of what motorcycle clubs were like from TV. I just didn't know how much of it was real and what all was exaggerated for ratings."

"What's the verdict?" King wondered, watching her thoughtfully.

"Depends on the answer to my question."

The corner of his mouth twitched, which was almost the same as a fucking belly laugh for our prez. "Probably a little of both, but leaning more toward serious. When it comes to my wife, I don't fuck around."

Impressively, Annika held his gaze for a long, intense interlude before cocking her head to the side. "I can respect that."

King raised a single eyebrow.

"My parents had a love like that," she added. "I hope I will too, someday."

The prez's eyes drifted to me, and his probing gaze made my skin crawl with the sensation that he was staring into my fucking soul. Then he looked back at Annika. "I'd bet on it."

Before the conversation could go any further, he changed the subject while stalking over to take a seat in front of Wizard. "Let's hear it," he ordered.

I gestured for Annika to explain, but she shifted

nervously, looking uncomfortable. King used one foot to shove an empty chair at me, and I nodded in thanks as I sat and pulled Annika onto my lap. She was stiff for about thirty seconds, then melted into me.

"Annika's parents died a couple of years ago and made her uncle her guardian," I began.

"They left me with our house, so he moved in with me," she said. I gave her a gentle squeeze, and she kept going. "I appreciated the gesture at the time, but it quickly became clear that he was more interested in free housing than me. I didn't really mind, though. I just wanted to get through the next couple of years, then I'd leave for college."

She went on to explain the details of her trust and how it was managed, finishing with what had happened that afternoon. By the time she was done, Wizard's fingers were already flying over his keyboard, and Ace was working on his phone, his brow furrowed in deep concentration.

I'd known they would have my back—and therefore Annika's. But sometimes, I was still surprised by the strength of a bond not forged in blood. Familial ties were always a big deal with Italian families, but when you threw the Mafia into the mix, the emphasis was even stronger. For fuck's sake, they called themselves "The Family." So it had been a culture shock when I'd first spent time with Mac and the Silver Saints. And even after years of being around MCs, there were times when I was reminded that the bond between my club brothers and me was often even more unbreakable.

"Digging into his finances now," Wizard commented distractedly. "I'll send 'em to Ace, then I'm gonna see what I can find in the dark corners."

"Got a contact at corporate for that bank," Ace muttered. "They'll be able to give us access to—" Ace broke off, and his head whipped up, his eyes going straight to Annika.

I gently set her on her feet and stood next to her. "Gonna let you get to it. Let me know what you find."

"I'll brief Ash in the morning," Blaze offered. "But he'll want to talk directly to Annika at some point."

As I ushered her to the door, I told him, "Took off the rest of the week to get shit straightened out."

King leaned back in his seat, his arms crossed over his chest as he watched me carefully. "Gonna call Rafa?" he asked just before I stepped into the hall.

I froze for a second, then squeezed Annika's

hand. When she looked up at me, I smiled gently. "Need to talk club business with my prez for just a sec. You okay out here?"

"Of course," she replied with a sweet smile.

"Thanks, baby."

After stepping back into the room, I shut the door behind me. Then I stared back at King and frowned. "Why?"

Since we didn't need the DeLuca Crime Family to handle club shit, I knew what he was really asking. But I played dumb because I didn't want to admit that I was a fucking idiot.

"Not about the uncle," he clarified, in an ironically cryptic response.

Sighing, I shook my head. "Not yet."

He raised an eyebrow and tilted his head.

"He'll tell my *mamma*," I admitted reluctantly.

Nothing else needed to be said. Every one of us knew that if Rafa told my *mamma* I'd met a girl, she'd be here with wedding dresses so fast our heads would spin.

"It's not like he can't keep a secret," Ace said, his tone sarcastic.

Yeah, this wasn't about my cousin, the Mafia underboss, not being able to keep information to himself.

"He'll do it just to fuck with me," I muttered, regretting my hasty actions at dinner the other night.

"Threw him under the bus at Sunday dinner, didn't you?" King stated.

King's uncanny ability to see what no one else could, particularly when people were trying *not* to say it, was seriously frightening sometimes.

When I didn't say anything, his mouth curled into an extremely rare smile. "Grandbabies."

"Fucking grandbabies."

"So give her what she wants," Blaze said, as if the answer were blatantly obvious, and I was too dense to figure it out.

"Working on it," I grunted.

King chuckled. "I'll send a vest to the shop for a property patch tomorrow."

I lifted my chin in thanks before doing a one-eighty and exiting the room.

Annika was leaning against the wall, reading something on her phone, and she had a frown on her beautiful lips.

"Problem?" I asked.

She popped her head up and gave me a tired smile. "Just thinking about my parents and how hard this would be on them."

Flipping her phone around, she showed me a

picture of a beaming couple with their arms around a younger Annika.

"Don't let this taint the happy memories, *dolcezza*," I murmured, pulling her into the circle of my arms.

She rested her cheek on my chest and sighed. "I don't even know how I'm going to face him when I get home."

"No fucking way are you going back to stay at that house, Annika," I growled, fisting her braid to tug her head back so I could look her in the face.

"I have nowhere else to go," she murmured distractedly.

The heat creeping into her ice-blue orbs nearly caused me to lose my concentration and kiss her. I released her hair and cleared my throat as I guided her head back to my chest.

"You'll stay here," I declared, the finality in my tone making it clear that there would be no arguing.

"Okay," she whispered.

5

ANNIKA

I couldn't believe I had just agreed to stay at a motorcycle club compound for the night. Maybe even longer, depending on how bad things ended up with Uncle Alec

My only excuse was that I was overwhelmed by learning what my uncle had been up to. Or at least that was the story I was sticking to because I wasn't ready to admit that a certain biker had brought my dormant libido roaring to life, which may have swayed my decision.

Being snuggled up against him wasn't helping either.

Wincing, I mumbled, "There's just one problem with this plan."

"What is it?"

"I don't have anything with me." I cringed as I thought about all the mementos I had at home. "And I don't like the idea of my uncle doing whatever he wants with the things that are most important to me. If he stole $50,000 from my trust, what's to stop him from rifling through my jewelry box and stealing all of the stuff my mom left me?"

"Is he there right now?" Matteo asked.

"I'm not sure."

"You got a security system with cameras? I can ask Wizard to hack into them to see if he's there," he offered.

Resisting the urge to ask him why his club had a lawyer, financial expert, and apparently also a hacker as members, I slapped my forehead with a groan. "Oh my gosh, why didn't I think of that myself? I have a door camera I can access on my phone."

He dropped his arms and stepped back—making me feel oddly bereft—so I could pull up the app on my phone. I was relieved to see that my uncle had left the house only fifteen minutes ago.

"Perfect," Matteo muttered. "If we're fast, we can grab your stuff before he gets back."

He led me outside to my Jeep—I was a little shocked that it had made it here so quickly—and opened the passenger side door for me. "It's better if we take your car. That way, if your uncle shows up and sees it in the driveway, he won't wonder what's going on until we're on our way out the door."

"Good idea," I agreed.

"Gimme the keys. I'll drive."

With my emotions in turmoil, I was in no condition to be behind the wheel, so I handed the fob over without any arguments. When he was in the driver seat, I gave him the address to my childhood home. Although it was on the other side of town, it only took about fifteen minutes to get there.

As we turned into the driveway, I pulled up the door camera app again to make sure Uncle Alec hadn't returned. "Looks like the coast is clear."

"Good," he grunted. "Let's move fast so you can get everything you need."

I raced inside and headed straight for my bedroom. Glancing over my shoulder, I asked, "Can you go to the kitchen and grab the recipe book in the drawer next to the stove? It's got all of my family recipes in it, and I have so many memories of my mom and grandma attached to it."

"Will do," he agreed. "Anything else you want from downstairs?"

I thought for a moment before answering, "Only

the photos of my parents that line the stairs and the one over the fireplace."

"I'll get them all," he promised.

I barely knew Matteo, but my gut told me that I could trust him to live up to his word. "Thank you."

While he took care of that, I grabbed my jewelry box and put it in my suitcase. Then I carefully took the garment bag with my mother's wedding dress from the hanger and placed it on top. Once that was done, I tossed in as much of my stuff as would fit before zipping up the bag and rolling it toward the door.

Matteo met me at the top of the stairs and grabbed the handle. "I have this. Everything else you asked for is already in the back of the Jeep."

"You moved fast."

"Didn't want to waste any time when we don't know when your uncle will be back."

As I followed him out the door, I took one last look inside the only home I had ever known. A tear spilled from my eye as I wondered if I would ever live here again or if my uncle's betrayal would make that impossible.

Matteo swiped his thumb across my cheek. "Your uncle is gonna pay for hurting you."

There was no mistaking the determination in his

voice, making butterflies swirl in my belly. "I don't know what I would have done without you today."

"That's not something you're gonna have to worry about from now on."

As I locked the door behind us, I asked, "What if Uncle Alec notices my stuff missing and covers up whatever he's done before we have a chance for your guys to figure out what happened?"

"Good point, *dolcezza*. Would he believe you if you sent him a text to let him know that you were staying with a friend for a few days?"

I shook my head, doing my best to hide my shiver of awareness over him speaking Italian again, even just one tiny word. "Only if it was Rachel, but she's in the Bahamas this week."

"Does your uncle pay close enough attention to know that?" he asked.

"Actually," I said thoughtfully, "he doesn't. As long as I am out of his hair, Uncle Alec doesn't ask too many questions."

"Go ahead and send him that text," he urged. "Hopefully, we'll get lucky, and it'll keep him off our backs until my brothers can take care of this shit."

I sent a quick message to Uncle Alec and heaved a deep sigh of relief that all of my favorite things were now beyond his reach. Matteo reached over to squeeze my thigh, and I pressed my hand over his to keep it there for the ride back to the compound.

When we pulled through the gate, he patted my leg before parking in a small lot to the left of the clubhouse. When I undid my seat belt and reached for the door, he murmured, "Wait for me to walk around to your side."

As he climbed out of the Jeep and grabbed my bag, I fanned myself. And not because it was a hot summer day.

I'd thought Rachel's teasing about me finding a hot tattoo artist to hold my hand was ridiculous, but she couldn't have been more right. Matteo had done a heck of a lot more than that for me.

Sliding my palm against his after he opened my door, I felt a ripple of awareness run through me. Our gazes met, and his bright blue orbs showed a hint of heat.

When he focused on my lips for a moment, I thought he might kiss me. But then someone called, "Need help, Ink?"

He helped me out of the Jeep before he looked over his shoulder and answered, "Yup."

The guy who rushed over wasn't wearing a leather vest like Matteo's. "What can I do for you?"

Matteo tossed my suitcase at him. "Bring this inside. You know where to put it."

He didn't give me the chance to ask where that was before he tugged me into the clubhouse, but I figured I'd find out soon enough. A place this big was bound to have plenty of rooms where I could crash while I figured things out.

When Matteo led me inside, Cerberus trotted toward us and gave me a thorough sniffing before laying on his back and offering me his belly. Laughing, I crouched down and scratched him behind the ears. "How are you, cutie?"

"Not sure anyone besides Stella has ever called him that before." Matteo shook his head with a laugh. "I was shocked to see him come right up to you earlier. Cerberus has never been one to take to new people, and he's only gotten more territorial since our prez and his old lady had their baby. He's protective as fuck over Cadell. I've barely seen him in this part of the clubhouse for the past four months since he likes to stick close to the baby."

"That's why he was here earlier? Since the baby was here with Stella?"

He nodded and watched Cerberus nudge my hand with his snout, begging for more affection.

"Only reason I can think of that he's here now is to see you," he mused. "Can't really blame him."

Matteo crouched down to scratch his neck. Then he leaned close and whispered something with a smug grin.

"What did you say?" I asked curiously.

Matteo winked at me before standing up and offering his hand to help me to my feet.

"That's between us men, baby," he replied with a sexy wink that had butterflies swirling in my stomach.

I was in the middle of a motorcycle club clubhouse, with a hot biker talking about babies while I petted a dog. Even though Cerberus looked as intimidating as his name, he wasn't at all what I would have expected for a pet that belonged to an MC. Then again, nothing had been what I expected since I walked through the door of Hellbound Studio. I was more okay with that than I probably should've been. Just incredibly tired from the emotional roller coaster.

"Do you mind if I lie down? Between pumping myself up for a tattoo that I didn't even get and finding out that my uncle has stolen from me, it's been a long day. I'm exhausted."

"Whatever you need, *dolcezza*."

6

INK

I wasn't sure what the fuck had come over me, but I'd been smug as shit when I told Cerberus that Annika would be sleeping in my bed tonight. Now, as I guided her over to the stairs, I tossed him another arrogant grin. Then I realized what I was doing and made a mental note to have one of the club's doctors examine my head.

We made our way upstairs and down the hall until we reached my room. Being an enforcer had its perks when it came to living at the clubhouse. My room was a good size and had its own bathroom. Although it wasn't permanently mine like the officers, so when I moved out, the spot would go to someone else.

Annika's gaze was full of open curiosity as she

looked around the room. "I wasn't sure what to expect," she said with a laugh.

"And?" I pressed as I shut the door behind us.

"I might have thought it would be a little messier," she admitted with a giggle. "Single guys and all that."

Laughing, I took her suitcase off the bed and moved it to a small couch in the corner. "Comes from being part of a big family, I suppose. You didn't put your stuff away. It wasn't your stuff anymore."

Annika laughed and plopped down on the end of the bed. "You live here, or it's just your room?" she queried, watching me open her bag and begin hanging her shit in my closet.

"I live here for now. The officers have what basically equates to an apartment, unless they live somewhere else. Then they still have a permanent room, but it's more like this one. I haven't needed more than this. There's a huge communal kitchen downstairs, and most of the old ladies take turns cooking for the club." I grinned and winked at Annika. "I do my fair share, though, because I couldn't leave my *mamma's* house without knowing how to make her special dishes. I'd go through withdrawals if I had to wait until I went home for her cooking."

As I'd hoped, her cheeks bloomed with pink, and her expression turned a little dreamy. "You cook?"

"My lasagna is fucking awesome," I boasted as I hung up the garment bag she'd brought and shut the closet door. It hit me then that I had no idea when she ate last.

"Are you hungry, baby? I can—"

She waved off my question and shook her head. "I know I should probably eat, but my stomach is in knots. And honestly, I'm so tired that I could probably go to bed for the whole night even though it's so early."

"Listen to your body, *dolcezza*," I encouraged, walking over to my dresser. "You had a fuck ton of emotional shit dropped on you today." After digging around in the top drawer for a few seconds, I found my smallest T-shirt and yanked it out. It would still be huge on her, but I needed to know she was sleeping in my clothes. "Go put this on, and I'll let you rest."

The last thing I wanted to do was tuck her into my bed and leave, but if I stayed, she wouldn't get any sleep, and I could see the toll the day had taken on her.

"I have—" she started to argue when I handed her my shirt.

"Just go get changed, Annika," I ordered.

She looked torn between doing as she was told and being stubborn, so I glided the pad of one finger along her jaw and inwardly smiled when she melted.

"Go on, *dolcezza*."

Silently, she stood and kicked off her shoes, then padded into the bathroom.

I turned down the bed, and when she came back into the room, all of my good intentions nearly went out the window. But I stuck to my guns and helped her get settled on the mattress.

"Don't go wandering outside the room without me, okay?" I pointed at her cell. "My number is in your phone. Text me if you need anything."

"You're not leaving, are you?" she asked, her tone betraying a hint of vulnerability.

"Just gonna get some work done while you rest. I'll be right downstairs if you need me."

"M'kay," she whispered, her eyelids already drooping.

Steeling myself against the onslaught of temptation I was about to be hit with, I bent over and kissed her on the forehead. Then I grabbed my cut and hot-footed out of there before her delicious scent broke my control.

Once I was in the hallway, I had to take a minute

and get myself under control. The last thing I needed right then was shit from my brothers because I was hobbling around due to the steel pipe between my legs.

My phone beeped, and I yanked it out of my pocket, expecting to see Annika's number, but it was Blaze.

There'd been a hiccup with our current job, and he needed me to fix it.

It wasn't well known—for good fucking reason—that the MC's main source of income revolved around making people disappear. Not like mercenaries or assassins, we didn't kill anyone without cause. But we would end their life in another way, for a healthy fee.

If someone could afford it, we'd erase their identity and help them establish a new life. The MC had kind of fallen into the work after helping out a few people as a favor. King had realized that making people disappear into a new life could be a very lucrative income stream, and several of the patches had abilities that were perfect for operations like this.

King's specialty was forging documents. Wizard was our computer genius. My gift as an artist came in handy outside the tattoo shop. We also taught the new patches skills that could help if they didn't come in with any talent, so we never lacked in the necessary areas to complete a job.

It certainly didn't hurt that I had connections with people who were some of the best smugglers in the world. The only reason I'd been willing to use that connection was because King had made it one hundred percent clear that it wasn't a condition to patch with the Hounds. Even though my being a member made them an ally to the boss, my cousin in New York, King always left the choice of involving The Family up to me. It was just another reason he had my complete trust and loyalty.

Our current job was a less common instance, though. One where we didn't require a fee because of the circumstances. Sometimes, we jumped in to simply help someone who desperately needed saving. But those situations were a well-guarded secret so we didn't get a fuck ton of sob stories from people who were trying to screw us over.

After sending Blaze a text that I was on my way, I headed to my studio in the clubhouse. They'd repurposed an office so that we could set up a room that had everything I needed to create whatever was required for each operation. One of the things that made me a unique artist was that my talents crossed over to mixed media. I was every bit as good at digital art as I was at drawing, painting, or tattooing. I could also sculpt and work with metal.

With all of my know-how, if I'd ever wanted to, I would have made incredible counterfeiting plates. It had been one of the reasons The Family had been so loath to let me out of their clutches. Thankfully, Nic wasn't interested in forcing people to work for him, and family came first to him...without the capital F.

Blaze and Cross were waiting for me when I arrived. "Got the car cleaned," Cross grunted as I opened the door to my studio. He was the club brother who managed our garage and was seriously fucking talented at scrubbing and chopping vehicles. "King was just finishing up some paperwork before delivering it all to the client."

"One of his tools busted," Blaze muttered. "We need you to hand draw it with your heated foil pen."

I stopped in my tracks and flipped around. "Are you fucking serious? With a foil pen? Do you have any fucking idea how stupid that idea is?" I was shouting by the time I finished.

Blaze winced. "Wow, I owe King a hundred bucks. He nailed your response verbatim."

Scowling, I ignored his comment and proceeded to explain exactly why this idea was ludicrous. "If I hesitate for even a single second, the machines will catch it as counterfeit. If by some miracle, I managed to finish the design without a hesitation mark, it would have to be perfect. No hesitation and not one mistake? And should the gods of fake identities be with us and those two things actually happened, it wouldn't matter because I don't have the right material."

Cross handed me a bag. "King said this should work."

I frowned as I opened the bag and took out the contents to examine it. It *could* work, but damn.

With narrowed eyes, I studied my brothers. "Why isn't he here asking me himself? Not like him to hide."

"Cadell is sick," Blaze explained.

Damn, that meant I couldn't be pissed that King wasn't there to yell at. This was one situation where I knew he'd allow me to let him have it because he knew, in the end, I'd give in and try.

"Fine, but tell him he owes me, so the next time I mouth off, it'll be a freebie."

Blaze pressed his lips together, clearly trying to hide a grin, tempting me to wring his neck. "Will do," he muttered. "What do you need to get this done?"

"Get the fuck out of my studio and don't let

anyone disturb me unless it's Annika, Ash, or someone who has anything useful to tell me about her situation."

Cross saluted me, and I punched him in the solar plexus. Watching him struggle to breathe made me feel better, so I went about gathering my shit, forgetting all about them.

The only good thing about the situation was that it would take my mind off the gorgeous temptation sleeping in my bed, wearing nothing but my shirt.

Apparently, the angels were on my side because I managed to complete the project on my third attempt.

I sent Blaze a text, hoping it would wake him since it was the middle of the fucking night. Then I decided to grab a snack.

Wizard's office door was open, so instead of walking by, I paused and glanced inside. He was intensely focused on his computer, but the second I stood in the doorway, he looked over at me.

"Finished it?" he asked, his brow practically in his hairline.

I nodded and scratched my chin, realizing I hadn't shaved in a couple of days. My chinstrap would soon be a beard if I didn't take care of that.

"Damn, kid. I'm impressed."

I snorted. "You and me both."

"Well, hopefully, the shit Ace and I have been digging up will brighten your day. But I still need some time to connect some dots."

"Ash won't be here until early afternoon, brother. Get some sleep."

"Yeah, I was headed home when I had a thought and just popped in to check it out."

"And what time was that?"

Wizard glanced at a clock and swore as he hopped up from his seat and started shutting everything down.

"In trouble with the missus?" I teased.

His expression softened in a way that it only ever did when he talked about his old lady. "Nah. She knows I get lost in my shit and loves me anyway." He shook his head as he shoved his wallet and keys into his pocket. "She's too fucking good for me. But I'm gonna keep her anyway."

I stepped back into the hall as he exited the office, then shut and armed the door.

"You really think you've found something?" I probed as we walked toward the lounge.

"Probably, but I wanted to be sure before we head down the road."

Sighing, I clapped him on the back. "I get it. But

just know, if I lose my mind while waiting and end up beating the shit outta you, it's your own damn fault."

Wizard snickered and turned toward the front door while I went through the swinging door near the bar that took me into the massive kitchen.

When the sun crested on the horizon, I had pancakes, French toast, four kinds of eggs, fried potatoes, grits, Italian sausage, and a fuck ton of other breakfast goodness ready for anyone who wandered in hungry.

After the first few guys stumbled in to eat before work, I trudged into the lounge and passed out on one of the couches for a couple of hours.

When I woke up, I hurried upstairs, worried that Annika was awake and feeling confined to my room all by herself. But she was still asleep, so to avoid climbing into bed with her, I grabbed some clothes and took a very cold shower.

"Good morning."

Her husky, sleep-warmed voice greeted me when I came back into the bedroom.

I sat down on the edge of the bed and did my best to keep my eyes on her face rather than perusing her body. "Morning, *dolcezza*. How are you?"

She shrugged. "I'm not really sure, if I'm being

honest. The rest did me some good, but I still feel emotionally drained."

I nodded and cupped her chin with one hand, brushing my thumb over her plump lips. "I get that. How about you take a shower, then we can snag some breakfast. Hopefully, someone will have something that will at least point us in a direction by then."

A small smile creased her lips, and she closed her eyes with a soft sigh.

Holy fuck. I made a vow to hear her make that sound again while I was buried deep inside her.

"That sounds wonderful," she told me sweetly, helping to distract me from the very dirty, very graphic images playing like a picture reel in my head.

While she was in the shower, I called King to talk with him about the project I'd completed.

Once we were both ready to go, I helped her put on my spare cut. Then I took her hand, and we walked downstairs together.

After we ate breakfast, I showed her my studio, careful to be vague about certain tools and projects. Since we'd gotten up late, it didn't feel like too long before Ace knocked on my door.

"Ash is here. Meeting with Prez."

Holding hands again, Annika and I hurried to meet my brothers in King's office.

Ash was at the conference table on the left side of the room, reading on his tablet, his face a mask of deep contemplation.

"Ash," I greeted. "This is Annika."

His head popped up, and he wiped the frustration from his expression as he greeted my girl. "Hey. I'm sorry it took me so long to get here."

Annika's face turned bright red, and she sighed. "No, I'm sorry. I had no idea that Matteo was going to drag you from your honeymoon! Your wife must hate me! I'm so sorry."

Ash grinned. "If we'd stayed, instead of coming back to help, my wife would have kicked my ass. So how about we just call it even and see how I can help?"

I shot him a grateful look as I took a seat across from him and tugged Annika down onto my lap. "Know you just got here, but have you come up with something?"

"Maybe. I think I might know where the loophole is that allowed your uncle to pull that money after you turned eighteen. Only from the checking account, though. Your investments are safe. But I need to do a little research in my law library. I also have a friend looking through some files at the Justice Department because I have a nagging feeling, and I've learned not to discount my hunches."

Annika pressed a hand over her heart. "Thank you." She sniffed and swiped a finger under one eye. "I don't know how to thank you."

Ash nodded absently, his mind already back on the documents he was reading on his tablet. "I think—"

His words were interrupted when Wizard and Ace marched into the room. "Got something," Ace announced, his tone packed with frustration.

"Haven't figured out all the details yet," Wizard muttered. "But we're close."

"To what?" I asked impatiently.

"Looks like Uncle Alec is in debt. *Big time.* He owes someone a couple of hundred grand, at least."

"You don't know who?" asked King.

"The trail is pretty well covered up," Ace replied. "Followed the money several times before I finally looked close enough in the right places to see a pattern. Then Wizard had to do some magic shit to literally follow the physical trail before I could come up with a theory. The best explanation I can come up with is bets placed by a bookie. Old school, though, the guy must use pen and paper because he's a fucking ghost."

"A bookie?" King tapped a finger on the top of his desk, his expression considering. "I might know someone who can help us find a local without a trace."

As conversation and ideas continued to flow in the room, I turned my attention to Annika. She'd been very quiet, her body resting against me as if she didn't have the energy to hold herself up.

"Hey, *dolcezza*," I murmured as I rubbed soothing circles on her back. "Doing okay?"

She nodded and finally sat up, giving me a pretty smile. "Yes. I'm overwhelmed, honestly."

"Overwhelmed?"

"I don't know how to thank all of you for helping me when you have no reason to."

I frowned and cupped her face between my hands. "There is nothing to say thank you for, baby. I take care of what's mine."

7
ANNIKA

Even though we'd only known each other for a day, hearing Matteo call me his sent a zing directly to my heart. And made my inner walls clench.

I'd never felt this kind of magnetic pull toward anyone before, so I wasn't sure if I should act on it or not. Or if I was imagining that Matteo felt it too.

I was pretty sure that he wouldn't say stuff like that if he wasn't attracted to me, but that didn't necessarily mean that he was going to do anything about it.

Matteo brushed his thumb under my right eye. "You look tired."

I shook my head with a soft laugh. "Are you trying to tell me that I look like crap?"

"Impossible." He sifted my hair through his fingers before letting it drop over my shoulder. "You're always fucking gorgeous, *bella*."

"You have to be careful about throwing around compliments in Italian," I warned, a sensual shiver racing up my spine.

His lips curved into a smirk. "Why's that?"

I rolled my eyes and playfully swatted at his chest. "As if you don't already know."

"Maybe I just wanted to hear you say it," he teased, his blue eyes filled with humor.

"Because a girl could get all kinds of ideas," I whispered.

"And if that's exactly what I want, *dolcezza*?"

"Then you should get a room," Ace suggested, reminding me that we weren't alone. A fact that I'd somehow managed to forget while we were surrounded by several of his club brothers.

Matteo pointed at him. "Just wait until it's your turn."

"His turn for what?" I asked as Matteo tugged me out of King's office, the guys' laughter drifting toward us.

"To find a woman of his own," he finally answered when we reached his room.

I wasn't sure if he meant that I was his for now,

or he had something more long-term in mind, but it didn't really matter to me right now. My world was whirling out of control, and Matteo was my much-needed anchor, keeping me from spiraling along with it.

"You want to take a nap?"

I looked up at him and shook my head. The tears I'd been holding back for too long finally spilled down my cheeks. Kicking the door shut behind us, he pulled me into his arms. Burying my face against his chest, I mumbled, "Sorry, I'm a mess."

"A beautiful one."

My laugh was watery as I tilted my head back. "So you're admitting that I'm a mess?"

"You have every right to be a little fucked up right now, Annika." He cupped my face and used his thumbs to brush my tears from my cheeks. "Gotta admit how impressed I've been with how you've held up, learning that you're only remaining family member betrayed you."

I sniffled. "And now here I am, crying about it."

"Never gonna complain or judge you for showing me your emotions, *dolcezza*. I want you to feel comfortable being vulnerable with me."

He brushed his lips against mine in a light kiss

that might have been meant to be comforting…except it quickly spiraled out of control.

A deep groan rumbled up his chest as he tilted my head back, my lips parting when his tongue swiped against them. I was breathless when he finally lifted his head again. His eyes were a deeper blue as he searched my expression before he pressed his mouth against mine again. He deepened the kiss, and sparks flew…straight to my core.

"Fuck, been wanting to do this for so damn long."

"So long?" I echoed with a giggle. "We only met yesterday."

"And it felt like for-fucking-ever."

I felt a feminine thrill at knowing I had that effect on Matteo. "Why?"

"Because I wanted you from the moment I heard you talking to Onyx. And I'm more than a little possessive, which was why I'm the only one who's gonna do your tattoo. I might not have ever felt like this before, but that's not gonna stop me from acting on it."

His confession gave me courage. "Then you shouldn't hold back with me. Go for it."

"You givin' me the green light, *dolcezza*?" he growled, one of his hands tangling in the back of my hair as his eyes burned into mine.

"Yes."

My voice was soft, but my one-word reply was enough for Matteo to pick me up and toss me on the mattress. I bounced a couple of times before he dropped next to me, his boots somehow off already. While he tugged my shoes from my feet, I dragged his leather vest down his broad shoulders.

The next few minutes were a flurry of kisses, touches, and tossed clothing. In barely any time at all, I was only in my bra and panties while Matteo was down to his boxer briefs, with his impressive bulge straining against them.

I'd never been naked—or even close to it—in front of a guy, let alone in bed with one before like this. But I didn't feel as self-conscious as I would've expected, not even when he was all lean muscle while I was extra curvy. I was too turned on to worry, as though the past twenty-four hours with Matteo had all been foreplay.

He undid the clasp on the back of my bra and slid the straps down my arms. My nipples pebbled under his stare. "Così bella."

I didn't speak Italian, but I knew enough to understand that he was saying something about me being beautiful. Reaching out to trace some of the black ink on his chest, I murmured, "You're not too shabby yourself."

"You like my tats?" he asked as he cupped the lush swell of my breasts.

I stroked the star on his right shoulder. "What's not to like? They're fantastic."

"Then you're gonna love when I do yours." His thumbs brushed over my nipples, making me shudder. "I drew most of mine."

"I'm looking forward to seeing what you come up with for me, but..." I let my words trail off as I squirmed.

"But you need something else from me right now?" he finished for me.

"Uh-huh," I breathed.

"And I'm gonna give it to you."

My inner walls clenched at the desire shining from his blue orbs, but then I froze up when I realized I needed to confess something to him before we went any further. "Um...I should...um...probably let you know that I've never done this before."

He froze, but the heat in his gaze intensified instead of disappearing. "You tellin' me that you're a virgin?"

"In every way." I swallowed the nervous lump in

my throat. "That kiss you gave me was the first real one I ever had."

"I hope you weren't expecting that to put me off because it only makes me want you more," he growled. "But I'll be as gentle as I can be, Annika."

"Don't hold back too much." I twined my arms around his neck. "I want you just the way you are."

"Thank fuck. 'Cause you're about to get all of me. Every single inch of my rock-hard cock is gonna be buried in your sweet pussy. Soon."

He didn't make me wait long to follow through on that promise. He laid me out on the center of the mattress before straddling my thighs. Then he cupped my breasts. "Your curves are even more mouthwatering than I thought they'd be. Which is saying a fuck of a lot because I knew they'd be fantastic."

Any lingering trace of doubt over my weight was wiped away from the pure masculine appreciation in his gaze. There was no missing that Matteo liked what he saw. A lot.

He kept his gaze locked on mine as he bent down to suck on my nipple. With each tug of his mouth, it felt as though a string was tied between my pebbled peak and my core. I arched my back to press my breast more deeply against his lips, and his deep chuckle blew against my sensitive skin as he shifted to the other side to pay it the same attention.

Once he had me writhing in need, he slid my panties down my legs. Then he spread my thighs wider to kneel between them. "Your curves are gonna be the death of me. So damn perfect."

"I'm glad you think so."

"Any man who doesn't is a damn fool," he growled, licking his lips as he stared between my legs. "Your pussy is even better."

He traced a thick finger around my lower lips before dipping the tip between them.

"Wow," I breathed, moving my legs to give him better access.

"Feel good?"

I pressed the back of my head against the pillow beneath it and gasped, "Uh-huh."

"It's about to get a fuck of a lot better."

He circled my clit, then moved lower to slowly push the tip into my channel, slowly working it inside me inch by inch. I was wet enough that it wasn't long before he was able to pump his finger in and out of me.

"Your pussy is so tight. It's gonna feel amazing when you're wrapped around my cock." My inner walls clamped around his digit. "You want that, don't you?"

My hips bucked off the mattress to meet the next thrust of his finger. "Yes, please. Yes."

"First, I gotta make you come." He lowered onto his stomach and wedged his shoulders between my thighs. "Get you all nice and slick so you can take me with a little less pain."

Then he started to devour me, using his tongue, lips, and teeth to drive me wild. "I'm so close."

He licked and bit at my clit while he worked another finger inside me. The brush of his whiskers against my sensitive skin only heightened my pleasure. I gripped the blanket in my fists while I writhed in his hold, my body tight. Then he pulled his fingers from me. My whimper of protest was replaced with a cry of satisfaction when he quickly replaced it with his stiffened tongue.

He ate me with reckless abandon until waves of pleasure crashed over my body. "Yes, Matteo! Oh yes!"

While my body was shuddering with my release, he got to his knees and shoved his boxer briefs down. His thick shaft sprang free, a bead of precome on the tip. I licked my lip, wondering what it tasted like, but then every thought flew out of my head when he notched himself at my center and pushed forward with one powerful thrust.

Anchoring his hard length deep inside me, he muttered, "*Mi dispiace, dolcezza.* I hate that I had to hurt you, but I'm gonna make it up to you with more pleasure than you can imagine."

After giving me a little time to adjust to his size, he asked, "Better?"

I gave my hips an experimental wiggle and was relieved to find there wasn't any pain, only pleasure. "Yeah."

"Thank fuck," he groaned before starting to move again.

The drive of his hips was slow at first, but he picked up the pace until he was practically pounding me into the mattress.

"Knowing this pussy is mine and only mine is hot as fuck."

"Yours," I gasped when he swiveled his hips on the next thrust.

"That's right, *dolcezza*. Mine."

Sliding his hands under my butt, he lifted me so he could go deeper, hitting my clit with every downward drive of his hips. I clutched at his biceps, my nails digging into his inked flesh hard enough to leave a temporary mark.

"Come for me again. Now."

Time hung suspended for a moment, and then the pleasure hit me. Even stronger than before. Waves and waves that felt as though they'd never end while he rode me through both of our releases.

When it was finally over, Matteo rolled onto his back and settled me against his chest. I felt as though my body was boneless, and I melted into his embrace —which was exactly where I wanted to be.

8

INK

"Rachel is back!" Annika squealed, bounding up to her knees and bouncing on the bed, making her big, sexy tits sway enticingly.

Her enthusiasm was contagious, and I laughed as I made a grab for her to yank her down so she was lying on top of me. "I like this look on you," I told her softly.

"What look? Naked and jumping around so I'm wiggling all my juicy bits?" Her peals of laughter rang throughout the room, and a wide grin split across my face.

"Juicy is fucking right, baby," I growled before flipping her onto her back and proceeding to show her just how delicious all her "bits" were.

After we'd showered and dressed for the day, I

remembered that I hadn't finished my thought earlier. I grabbed her hand and shuffled her into the bathroom to stand in front of the mirror, then slipped my arms around her, resting them on her soft, sexy belly.

"As much as I enjoyed seeing all those delicious curves up close, that wasn't what I meant earlier."

She blinked at me in confusion.

"The look I like on you is happiness, *dolcezza*. I love seeing you happy."

Annika's expression turned soft, and her body melted back against me. "Then don't go anywhere," she whispered with a sweet smile. "Because you make me deliriously happy."

"Same, *dolcezza*. Same."

I'd have kept her glued to me twenty-four seven if I could have, but I couldn't refuse her request to go have coffee with Rachel when she looked so delighted about it. Not when I had no legitimate reason to say no.

I kissed the fuck out of her before buckling her into the driver's seat of her Jeep. "Be careful and protect what's mine," I ordered gruffly before capturing her lips one more time.

"You aren't going to convince me to cancel with those tempting lips and that growly voice if that's what you're trying to do," she muttered, sounding less than confident.

I grinned but took a step back. "Go, *dolcezza*. Before I change my mind and drag you back to my cave to have my wicked way with you."

She glanced between me and the clubhouse, appearing even more indecisive after my comment. As much as I wanted to take advantage of the moment, I was more interested in fucking her after she came home and was still glowing with happiness.

I was saved from ruining my good intentions when Onyx stuck his head out of the door and shouted, "Ink! Waiting on you, man."

"Have fun, baby. Be careful."

"Okay. See you soon."

I watched her drive away, then tromped back to the front door, my mood already shit by the time I stepped inside. Onyx was waiting, and we hopped into my truck and drove out to Hellbound Studio.

I had no reason for wanting to keep her locked in my room—beyond my desire to tie her to the bed naked so I could fuck her until we both passed out from the ecstasy—but something was nagging at me. A dark feeling in my gut that I shouldn't have let Annika out of my sight.

Since she had made plans with her friend, I'd

had Onyx rebook a couple of my clients, but it probably hadn't been the best idea. Luckily, I was excellent at my job and didn't need to be at full concentration to do my best. But with my mind somewhere else, and that gnawing feeling eating away at me, it felt like a whole day had gone by when my phone buzzed in my pocket.

Taking it out, I saw Annika's picture on the screen, and I quickly answered it. "Hey, *dolcezza*," I greeted, my mood already lifted. "How was your coffee?"

"Um...so, don't freak out, okay?"

"Annika?" I growled. "What the fuck happened?"

My gut clenched, insisting that I'd been right and shouldn't have let her go.

"I'm fine. Really. I swear. It was just a small accident."

"Onyx!" I bellowed as I spun around and marched into the office where he was doing paperwork. "Call Cross at Inferno and tell him to bring a tow truck to—where are you, Annika?"

She sighed and gave me the nearest intersection, which I relayed back to Onyx.

"I'll meet him there," I finished as I jogged out to my truck.

Once I was seated and the vehicle started, I connected the phone to the Bluetooth and pulled out of the parking lot. "Tell me everything, Annika."

While I drove to her, she relayed everything that had happened.

Other than the fact that the driver had taken off right after hitting her, it sounded like it had truly been a random accident. But I wasn't completely convinced.

A tow truck with the Inferno Cycles and Customs brand emblazoned on the side pulled up just as I arrived. I parked far enough away to give him plenty of room to maneuver Annika's Jeep, then climbed out of my truck and jogged over to the corner where she was talking with several police officers.

As soon as she saw me, she ran straight into my arms. "I'm okay," she said, her voice muffled against my chest. "Really, Matteo. I'm not hurt, and the car doesn't have a lot of damage."

I couldn't speak yet. I just stood there and held her, trying to calm my racing heart.

"Matteo?" she finally asked after a period of silence.

"What did the police say?" I grunted, shifting

her to my side so I could talk to them when they approached.

"Ink," one of the cops greeted me.

"Daniel," I replied. Daniel was a friend, if you could call it that, to the Hounds. He'd helped us out from time to time with information. His partner, Harry, was an old guy and a stickler. He was very old school, though, which meant he was a pain in the ass.

But I still greeted him cordially. No reason to make an enemy. "Harry."

"This your girl?" he asked, his expression gentle when he looked at Annika.

"Mine," I confirmed with a sharp nod.

"Got here quick," he grunted. "Good man."

I raised an eyebrow at Daniel, and he mouthed, "Reminds him of his granddaughter."

"I tried to tell him I'm okay," Annika insisted with a sigh.

Harry frowned at her. "Doesn't matter. When a man's woman is in trouble, he should be there for her. From the way he's protecting you, I'd say you got yourself a decent fella, miss."

Daniel suppressed a grin, but I wasn't about to risk any ground I'd gained with Harry by coming off at all disrespectful.

"Thank you for watching her until I could get here," I said with genuine gratitude.

"Of course. Now, I'd like to go over it one more time, miss. In case you think of anything else that could help us track down the reckless bastard who ran you off the road."

By the time we finished speaking with the police, Cross had collected Annika's Jeep, and we were left alone next to my truck.

"I don't like it," I muttered.

"I wouldn't like it if you were in an accident either, Matteo. But life—"

"No. I mean, this doesn't feel right," I told her as I walked her around to the passenger side. "I'm not convinced it was an accident."

Annika eyed me with confusion as I helped her up into her seat. "What else would it be? It's not like someone would have hit my Jeep on purpose."

"Gonna put Wizard on it anyway," I mumbled before slamming her door shut and stalking around to the other side of the truck. Once I'd climbed inside, I turned over the engine and pulled away from the curb. "Until we know for sure, you're not leaving my side."

Annika huffed. "You can't just lock me up in your bedroom, Matteo."

A wicked smile curled my lips. "Was that a challenge, *dolcezza*?"

"Um...no," she answered hesitantly. Then she squirmed in her seat and breathlessly asked, "But what if it was?"

"Oh, *dolcezza*," I crooned. "Then I'm up for it."

The double entendre wasn't lost on her.

9
ANNIKA

Being confined to the Hounds of Hellfire clubhouse should've been a punishment, except I spent most of the past two days in bed with Matteo. I couldn't complain too much when he gave me more orgasms than I could count, fed me delicious food I didn't have to cook, and talked me into taking plenty of naps so I was well-rested for our next round of sex. It was better than any vacation I'd ever taken, but I had reached the point where I missed being outside.

"Pretty please," I begged, pressing my palms together while I widened my eyes with a pleading expression. "We don't know that my accident was anything more than whoever hit me getting freaked out because they don't have insurance, and that's why they drove off. And the compound is surrounded by an electric fence. I'll be perfectly safe if I go outside for a breath of fresh air."

I loved how protective Matteo was over me. I didn't feel suffocated by how he was because it had been so long since anyone looked out for me the way he did. Having someone in my life—besides Rachel—who truly cared meant the world to me.

"Shit." He scrubbed his palm across his chinstrap beard and sighed. "I guess we can have lunch on one of the tables out back. We're surrounded by woods on that side."

"Like a picnic," I squealed, clapping.

"Yeah, we can do that if that's what you want, *dolcezza*."

I bounced on my heels. "I do."

Matteo and I headed into the kitchen to make sandwiches, grab a bag of chips, and pour ourselves a couple of drinks. Then we headed out back to the yard behind the addition to the clubhouse where King, Stella, and Cadell lived.

"Life is good." The sun was shining, Matteo had me as close as I could be without sitting on his lap, and our lunch was simple but delicious.

He brushed a quick kiss against my lips. "I have no complaints."

I took another bite of my turkey club. "Mmm."

Matteo chuckled and wiped a bit of mayonnaise from the corner of my mouth, then licked it from his thumb. "Delicious."

"Remind me to add extra to yours the next time we make sandwiches." I bumped my shoulder against his.

He winked. "Tastes better when it comes from your sweet lips."

"You say the nicest things."

He grinned at me. "Only because you make it easy. Never been like this with anyone but you."

That was another thing I appreciated about Matteo. He just put his feelings for me out there without trying to play any games. Which was great since I'd be at a huge disadvantage if he did.

I enjoyed the fresh air as we finished our meal. While we were cleaning up our mess, Matteo bent down to pick up a paper towel that had dropped on the ground. There was a loud, unfamiliar crack of noise, and then I felt a sharp sting on the fleshiest part of my arm.

I didn't understand what was happening, but he quickly sprang into action, gently pulling me to the ground before rolling us under the table we'd just used for our picnic.

"What the heck was that?" I asked, reaching over with my good hand to touch the spot on my arm that was throbbing.

"Gunshot."

My eyes widened at his one-word answer, and then I gasped when I looked down at my fingers and saw blood on them. "I think I might have been shot."

"Fucking hell," he growled, levering himself up enough to sweep his gaze over my body. A muscle jumped in his jaw as he spotted the blood on my arm.

"You can say that again," I grumbled.

"It's gonna be okay, baby," he promised.

I flashed him a weak smile. "I know you'll keep me safe."

"Not sure I deserve your faith in me when I didn't protect you."

"This isn't your fault," I insisted. "If anyone is to blame, it's me. I'm the one who talked you into having lunch out here."

"Nobody should have ever been able to get to you. We're on Hounds property, for fuck's sake."

Footsteps thundered on the ground, and then I saw boots surrounding the table. King bent down, and his face was only inches from mine. "You guys okay?"

"No, we're not fucking okay. My woman was shot," Matteo growled.

Ash called, "Nora's inside. She can take a look at Annika once Kevlar and Rebel confirm that it's safe."

"Tell them to hurry the fuck up," Matteo demanded, keeping his body over mine.

"They know what's riding on their sweep of the woods," King murmured. "Nobody's gonna let that asshole get another shot at your woman."

"Appreciate it, Prez, but she needs to get inside so Nora can take a look at the damn bullet wound in her arm," Matteo muttered.

"Soon."

The next few minutes felt as though they took forever while I waited under the table with the man I'd fallen head over heels for on top of me, his big hand wrapped around my arm. Finally, King told us it was safe to come out, and Matteo carefully climbed off me and helped me get out. He stayed directly behind me as we hurried into the clubhouse, where he led me through a hallway I hadn't gone down before and into a medical clinic I didn't even know was here.

Nora, Ash's wife, was waiting for us. She quickly ushered me over to an exam table. "Help her up here."

Matteo lifted me off my feet and set me on the padded surface. Then he moved to stand by my uninjured side, interlacing our fingers as he slid his other arm behind me.

Nora asked me a bunch of questions, checked my vitals, then took a closer look at my arm.

"Thank goodness, this isn't as bad as it looks." She applied pressure over the spot where I'd been shot and lifted my arm in the air.

"Did she lose too much blood?" Matteo asked.

Nora shook her head. "She'd be lightheaded if that was a problem, and judging by the gash in her arm, the bullet only grazed her."

Just hearing her say that eased some of the pain and most of my tension. "See, it's just a graze. I'm okay."

"Nothing is okay about this situation!" The vein in Matteo's temple visibly throbbed.

"At least she's accepting medical treatment for her minor gunshot wound," Nora muttered, shooting a loaded glance at Ash, who'd followed us into the clinic. "Unlike someone else I know, who had a freaking bullet in his arm and refused to let me get a good look at it or take him to the hospital."

I twisted around to gawk at Ash. "You got shot and refused treatment? For more than just a graze?"

"I wouldn't put it that way," he disagreed. "I just put it off until I could get to the clubhouse so Razor could take care of it for me."

I quirked a brow at Nora as she cleaned my wound. "I bet that went over well with you."

Ash snorted. "She was pissed as fuck and made me work hard to get her to agree to a date."

"Which he then blew off for club business," Nora grumbled with a roll of her eyes.

They seemed so madly in love with each other, it was difficult to believe they'd started off so rocky. "Really?"

"Yup," Nora confirmed.

After she finished bandaging my arm, Ash wrapped his arms around her. "Luckily, she gave me another chance, and I proved to her that I wouldn't fuck up again."

"Aw," I sighed.

Wizard poked his head into the clinic. "You got a second?"

Matteo shook his head. "Not gonna leave my woman's side until she's taken care of."

"You heard Nora. I barely got shot. I'm fine."

Wizard shook his head. "That's not good enough for you, is it?"

"Not a chance in hell," Matteo confirmed with a slight nod.

Ash tugged Nora from the room.

Wizard's gaze slid toward me, and he must've found whatever he was searching for in my expression because he came into the room. Hooking his foot around the leg of the rolling stool Nora had used when she examined me, he rolled it close and sat down. "This is more about Annika than club business, so I guess I can share the news in front of her."

Tension filled my body, and my muscles locked. "What is it?"

Matteo threaded his fingers through mine as Wizard announced, "Your uncle is on the run."

My shoulders slumped as relief coursed through my veins. "Well, at least he can't come after me if he's gone."

Unfortunately, I underestimated the lengths my uncle would go to.

10

INK

I was just about to take Annika back up to our room when Kevlar popped his head into the clinic. His gaze met mine, and he jerked his chin toward the hallway.

"Need to talk to Kevlar for a second, *dolcezza*. You good?"

Annika sighed in exasperation, but there was a little humor in her ice-blue depths. "I'm more than fine, Matteo. Stop worrying so much."

"Not gonna happen," I muttered before giving her a quick kiss and following Kevlar out of the room.

Rebel was waiting for us in the hallway, and his expression was furious.

"Show him," Kevlar grunted, and Rebel held up a bullet.

"You found it?"

Kevlar nodded. "Found the casing in the woods, too." He opened his fist to show it to me, and my eyes narrowed.

"Are those fucking custom?" I growled.

"Yup," Kevlar replied.

"Son of a bitch." More than likely, this meant we were dealing with a professional. "How the fuck did they miss?"

Rebel handed Kevlar the bullet, then shoved his hands into his pockets as he leaned back against the wall. "Wooded area around the compound is tough to navigate, and we patrol it regularly. Probably couldn't find a decent perch."

"So we got damn lucky."

Rebel nodded.

Which meant we probably wouldn't be so fortunate a second time.

"I don't recognize the style." Kevlar took a closer look at the components. "But my connections in that world only go so far…"

He left the rest of his thought unsaid, knowing I'd understand.

Scowling, I muttered, "How have I become even more involved with The Family since I left them behind?"

I yanked my cell phone from the inner pocket of my cut and pulled up Rafa's number.

"Matteo," he greeted when he picked up.

"Need a favor," I grumbled.

"You already owe me," Rafa replied smoothly, not bothering to hide the smugness in his tone.

"Debatable. We can get into that shit later. Someone is trying to kill my woman, and you're better equipped to find the bastard than I am."

"How can I help?" All traces of humor were gone now.

"Pretty sure it's a pro."

"And that's more my world than yours," Rafa concluded.

"Fair assumption," I agreed.

"What makes you think it's a hitman?"

"Custom ammunition, mostly. But more specifically, the style of it," I explained.

"You don't recognize a signature?"

"No."

"*Capisco.* Text me photos, but I'll send a soldier to collect it for closer examination," he offered. "If they're local, Domenico might know of them."

Domenico DeAngelis had been my first thought as well. He was one of The Family's best assassins.

"*Bene. Apprezzo il tuo aiuto,*" I murmured, thanking him for his help.

"*Sicuramente.* I'll be in touch."

After hanging up, I filled in Rebel and Kevlar, then returned to the clinic exam room.

Wizard watched me curiously, and I thought about his earlier comment. Club business versus what Annika should be allowed to know.

"Think it's a pro," I grunted. "Rafa is on it."

"The Family?" he asked, his brow shooting up.

I nodded sharply. "Whatever it takes."

He glanced at my girl before meeting my eyes again. "King gave approval to tell her whatever you think she needs to know, as long as it doesn't compromise club business. He suggested you start with The Family."

"Your family?" Annika asked.

Wizard clammed up and jumped to his feet. "Gonna leave you two to talk." He walked to the door, but he slowed as he passed me and murmured, "If she can handle club life, she can handle knowing about your blood ties."

He was right, but that didn't make me feel a fuck of a lot better about telling my sweet, innocent Annika that her man was technically a member of The DeLuca Crime Family.

"You need to rest, *dolcezza*." I held out my hand, and she grabbed it, allowing me to help her to her feet. "Let's go back to the room, and we'll talk."

She frowned but didn't say anything as we walked back to my quarters.

I waited until I was seated on the couch with Annika in my lap before starting, "You know I live my life in the gray area. My hands are dirtier than you'll ever know the full extent of. And there will be many times when I can't share things with you."

Annika smiled softly, then laid her head on my shoulder and slipped her arms around my torso. "I know. But I also know what a good man you are."

She gave me a gentle hug, and I sent up a prayer to Santa Rita da Cascia that knowing about my connection to The Family wouldn't tip the scales in the wrong direction.

"You know my last name is DeLuca. Like the crime family."

"I already assumed you were distantly related or something like that," she replied, raising her head so we were face-to-face.

"Not distantly, *dolcezza*. The boss, Nic DeLuca, is my cousin. His father, mine, and Rafa's—the underboss here in the south—were brothers. I was born and raised in New York until I was ten."

"You're a member of the Mafia?" she clarified with a double blink.

"No, I'm a member of the Hounds of Hellfire. But I have blood ties to the Mafia." I went on to give her a brief summary of my background, my connections to the DeLucas, as well as my history with the Silver Saints and now the Hounds.

To my relief, she listened quietly, seeming to simply absorb the knowledge rather than recoil from it.

When I was finished, she chewed on her lip for a moment, then asked, "What you said about a pro? You meant a hitman?"

I nodded.

"And you thought it was more likely that your cousin would be able to identify a hired killer than the MC?"

I nodded again.

"That was really smart, Matteo. I wouldn't have thought of that." She chuckled. "But then, these worlds are all new to me."

Part of me was glad she seemed to be in full acceptance of everything I'd told her, but the other part...

"I hate that you're being exposed to such ugliness," I admitted. "But it's my life, and I'm too selfish to let you go. I promise to shield you as much as I possibly can, though."

Annika frowned and placed a palm on my cheek. "I know there are plenty of things I can't know, but I don't want you to treat me like some angel on a pedestal. I want to be your partner. For you to be able to be vulnerable and honest with me, just like you asked me to be with you."

"You're so fucking incredible." Sighing, I rested my forehead against hers and closed my eyes. "How did I get so damn lucky?"

"You must have done something redeemable," she teased with a giggle.

My body was on fire, and my gaze was heated when I raised my head and met her gaze. "Maybe, but wicked is all that's left, baby."

I surged to my feet and tossed her on the bed, then proceeded to prove just how sinful I could be before we fell asleep in an exhausted heap.

When I woke up from our nap, Annika's warm, soft body was pressed against me, and I buried my face in her silky, dark blond tresses. *Damn, she was amazing.*

It seemed impossible that she had accepted me for who I was and wanted to be with me despite knowing that my hands would often be dirty with more than just tattooing ink.

Even though it had only been a few days, I couldn't imagine going to bed without her in my arms. Annika was the shining spot in a life filled with a lot of darkness. She had already become more vital to me than oxygen. She was the love of my life, and I was gonna make that official the second we'd taken care of the shit hanging over us because of her bastard uncle.

However, considering I hadn't used protection even once since I popped her cherry, I could already have accomplished one of my goals. Still, I should up my chances...and even after it happened, we'd need plenty of practice for the next one.

My arms closed even tighter around Annika, cuddling her incredible curves closer to me. I fucking loved that she wasn't so tiny that I felt like I might break her. She was soft and strong at the same time. And fuck, her tits, hips, and ass were sexier than I'd ever imagined a woman could be. I practically walked around with a permanent semi because she was never far from my thoughts.

She stirred in my arms and shifted around to face me. Her lids lifted slowly and she looked up at me with adorable, sleepy eyes. Her pale blue orbs looked like ice, but they were filled with warmth.

"*Ciao, dolcezza,*" I mumbled before burying my face in her neck and taking a deep breath. Something about her sweet scent soothed me every time I inhaled it. I glided one hand up from her hip to rest just below her tits as I placed tiny kisses on the sensitive skin of her throat. She shivered, and I grinned, loving how much I affected her.

"*Ciao,*" she replied in a shy, breathy tone.

I brought my head back up and gazed down into her face. "I get it," I told her as I stared at her perfect mouth.

"Get what?"

"Why you think it's so fucking sexy when I speak to you in Italian."

A pretty blush stole across her cheeks, and she giggled. "You'll have to teach me more."

"Happy to, baby. As long as you promise to never speak Italian in front of another man."

She laughed, but it trailed off when she clocked my serious expression. "Never?"

I shook my head. "They'd try to steal you, and I'll kill anyone who tries to take you away from me."

"But what if—"

"Annika," I growled. "I'm warning you, baby.

That would be the fastest way to earn yourself a cherry-red ass."

When her expression turned intrigued, I groaned. "The threat is ruined if you're hoping for a spanking, *dolcezza*."

She flushed and smiled at me sheepishly.

Unable to help it, I laughed and kissed her softly. I'd meant it to be quick, but heat exploded between us, sizzling over my skin and sending streaks of desire straight to the big, thick rod poking her in the stomach.

I rolled her to her back before covering her curvy body with my own. Electricity sparked wherever we touched. My groin nestled into hers, pressing my hard erection into the heat of her pussy. She was fucking drenched, and my cock easily slid between her folds as I shifted to settle more fully against her. She arched her back and moaned, causing my dick to swell impossibly bigger.

Lazily, I rocked against her, gliding through her juices again, making sure to rub over her clit with each pass. Her needy little noises drove me out of my fucking mind.

"You need to come, *dolcezza*?" I rasped.

She whimpered and nodded frantically. "Please, Matteo."

"Piacere mio." I dipped my head down to take one of her fat nipples in my mouth as I increased my pace. The heat of her pussy and slick coating of her arousal on my cock was straining my control.

"Matteo," she moaned as her head thrashed from side to side. Her legs circled my hips, and she bucked up to meet my shallow thrusts. "More," she begged softly.

I rubbed harder and switched my attention to the other breast.

"No," she gasped as I dragged my cock over her clit. "Inside me. Please."

I let her nipple go with a pop and grunted, "Fuck, baby."

"That's the point," she uttered with a cute little smirk.

I chuckled and dropped a kiss on her lips before pulling back, then shifted as I slid forward so that the tip of my cock teased her entrance. "You want my cock, *dolcezza?*"

"Yessss," she moaned, her hands tunneling into my hair and clenching the strands in a tight grip.

I was barely inside her, but her walls clenched and massaged the tip of my cock, draining all my blood in my body to my shaft as pleasure rocketed through me.

Finally, I surged forward, burying myself to the hilt. "Oh, fuck!" I shouted.

Annika screamed, her head thrown back in ecstasy as she clamped down on my dick like a vise.

"Oh, Matteo, yes! Don't stop!!" she demanded, turning me on even more.

"*Si, dolcezza,*" I groaned before withdrawing all the way and slamming back in. "Shit! Oh, baby, yes! Fuck! Love this tight little pussy. Fuck! Oh fuck, yeah."

After a few more hard thrusts, I withdrew slowly, stopping when only a few inches remained inside her. Then I grasped her legs and untangled them from around me, shifting so I was straddling her. I closed her thighs around my cock, causing her to grip me even tighter.

"Press those legs closed, *dolcezza*," I ordered. "Want you to fight it when I pull out. Keep my cock inside you."

She stared up at me and licked her lips. Then her walls spasmed, and black spots danced in front of my eyes. I caught her wrists in my hands and laced our fingers together before raising her arms over her head and pressing them into the mattress.

I started to move again, and she obeyed my command, fighting me every time I withdrew. It wasn't long before we were both panting wildly, our bodies slapping together as we bucked, meeting each other thrust for thrust.

Eventually, my control deserted me, and I pounded in and out of her tight pussy, hard and fast. "Oh, fuck yeah! That's it, baby. Take me even deeper. Fuck yes! Fuck!"

Annika screamed one last time as her orgasm crashed into her. Her pussy walls rippled, triggering my climax. I shoved in hard, seating myself as deep as possible so the tip of my dick bumped her cervix. Then I bellowed her name as I came long and hard, filling her with my hot seed.

"Damn, *dolcezza*. If this just keeps getting better, it's gonna kill me."

I panted as I released her hands and collapsed on top of her. But I worried about my weight crushing her, so I lifted my body until her arms curled around me and held on.

"Don't move yet," she murmured softly. "You feel so good. And with everything..."

She'd averted her eyes, so I gently took hold of her chin and forced her to meet my gaze. "Tell me, *dolcezza*."

A pretty blush stained her cheeks. "You...you make me feel so safe like this."

I took her lips in a tender kiss, then gave her a lopsided smile. "If this makes you feel safe and secure, I'm more than happy to keep you under me as often as possible."

Annika laughed, and her joy spread warmth around my heart. Those three little words almost popped out right then, but I didn't want that moment tainted by the threat hanging over her.

11

ANNIKA

I had barely caught my breath from our lovemaking when Matteo's phone rang. "Shit, gotta take this."

I pulled the sheet over my breasts after he twisted around to grab his phone from the bedside table. "Ink."

I only caught a few low words from the other end of the call, and then Matteo hissed, "Shit."

He listened for another moment. "Thanks, *cugino*. At least this solves one of my woman's problems."

I perked up at that, scrambling to my knees while I waited for Matteo to finish his call. After he said his goodbyes, I asked, "What did you find out?"

"The reason your uncle stole from you...tried to

hurt you." He scraped his palms over his face with a deep sigh. "It's because he's got a gambling problem."

"Oh." I didn't understand why he seemed so bothered by the news when it certainly wasn't any worse than what we'd already learned about Uncle Alec. "Is it really bad?"

"Depends on how you look at it," he grumbled, shaking his head. "You know how I told you that my family is Mafia?"

I giggled and nodded. "Um, yeah. Those orgasms you gave me didn't completely wipe out all of my brain cells, and it's not something I'm likely to forget."

"They're the ones he owes the money to."

"Ahh, I get it now." I shuffled closer and wrapped my arms around him. "Nothing my uncle did is your fault. Or your family's. It's all on him."

"I'm lucky you're so damn sweet." He brushed a kiss against my temple.

I tipped my head back to smile at him. "And I'm lucky that you're...you."

He captured my mouth in a deep kiss that left me wanting more when he finally ripped his mouth from mine. "You have no idea how much I want to spread you out on this mattress and take you again."

"Do I get a vote?" I wagged my brows. "Because I like the sound of that."

"Sorry, *dolcezza*. I hate to leave you when you've just learned that your bastard of an uncle owes money to my family, and that's why he's pulled all of this shit." He stroked his thumb against my cheekbone. "But I need to take care of something urgent. If it could wait..."

"Then you wouldn't go," I finished for him with a soft smile. "I know that."

"Like I said, you're too damn sweet."

I winked at him. "You can make it up to me later."

Lying back on the mattress, I curled against Matteo's pillow while I watched him get ready. It was a show I would've gladly paid for, even more so when he was taking his clothes off instead of putting them back on his gorgeous, tattooed body.

When he was done, he gave me another kiss before he walked out of the room.

He left his extra leather vest for me, like he'd done every day since we met. I tugged it over my outfit with a smile before heading downstairs to see who was around.

It was impossible to feel lonely around here

because there was always someone to hang out with. Not that Matteo had left my side often.

Another thing I loved about staying at the clubhouse was that nobody minded if I used the big kitchen. And there always seemed to be someone there who enthusiastically volunteered to eat whatever I made.

Today, I found a trio of pregnant women at one of the tables when I walked into the kitchen. "If I didn't know better, I'd think there was something in the water around here."

"In the water?" Violet asked, her brows drawing together.

Thea pointed at her still flat belly. "Yeah, to get knocked up."

Courtney snorted. "If Ink is anything like his club brothers, he doesn't need water to make that happen."

My cheeks filled with heat as I hurried over to the pantry to peek inside.

"I'm going to take that as a yes...Ink is very much like the rest of the guys around here after they've claimed us," Violet teased.

Echo glared at his wife and growled. "No thinking about what any other man gets up to in bed."

"That's not what I was doing," Violet huffed.

"We were just kidding around with the new girl," Courtney chimed in.

"Yeah," Thea agreed with a nod.

Onyx shook his head and laughed. "Gotta love how the sisterhood sticks together around here."

Violet crossed her arms over her chest. "Are you making fun of us?"

"He better not be," Echo warned.

Before the conversation spiraled out of control, I called, "Anyone in the mood for a fresh cobbler?"

"Me," they all yelled back in unison.

I had only been staying at the Hounds of Hellfire compound for less than a week, but I already felt more at home here than I had in my own house since my parents died. It had taken everything that had come to light about my uncle for me to finally realize he had tarnished so many happy memories of my childhood home. My dad was probably rolling over in his grave due to how his brother treated me.

The last time I cooked anything from my mom's family recipes was less than a month after their accident. I made my grandmother's famous peach cobbler with homemade vanilla bean ice cream and had been so excited to share it with Uncle Alec.

But his reaction was the opposite of what I

expected. His nose scrunched as though he smelled something bad, and he made a tsking sound. "You really should pay closer attention to what you eat, Annika. It would be a shame if you gained any more weight."

My parents had always told me how beautiful I was, so his words had come as a shock. From that point on, I never baked another dessert. Until today.

I pulled several large cans of fruit out of the pantry. "It's better with fresh peaches than canned, but I can make do with these."

"There's a big bag of Bing cherries in the fridge." Courtney stood and crossed the room to dig through the produce bin for them. "I had a craving for them a few days ago, so Pax stocked up in case I wanted them again."

"Only so he wouldn't be stuck going out for them in the middle of the night," Onyx mumbled.

I pointed a wooden spoon at him. "Keep riling the pregnant women up, and you won't get any cobbler."

He pretended to zip his mouth shut and toss away the key, making me giggle. Then I got to work on making three kinds of cobbler—peach, cherry, and a mixture of both. When I pulled them out of the oven, I felt closer to my mom, knowing I did her recipe justice.

"Who wants a piece?"

Once again, everyone in the kitchen yelled, "Me," in unison.

I dished up six plates. "Next time, I'll make some homemade ice cream to go with this. Luckily, we had a tub of vanilla in the freezer that I could use."

Matteo's club brothers and their women were much more appreciative of my efforts than my uncle had been.

"If this tastes as good as it smells, you're not going to get a single complaint about the perfectly fine ice cream in the freezer," Courtney assured me.

"Holy fuck, this is amazing," Onyx mumbled around a spoonful.

"Mm-hmm," Violet agreed.

Echo flashed me an appreciative smile after seeing how much his wife was enjoying the cobbler, then took a bite of his and murmured, "Damn good."

Thea just nodded and spooned another bite into her mouth.

The kitchen was quiet while we all polished off our servings. Onyx was the first to finish. He patted his stomach with a wide grin. "I gotta admit, I appreciate the benefits that come with my brothers claiming their old ladies."

"What the fuck did you just say?" Echo demanded, glaring at him.

Onyx held his hands up in a gesture of surrender. "I meant the food, man."

"Then get your own woman," Echo grumbled.

Onyx shook his head. "Not anytime soon."

I found myself hoping that Matteo's friend had just tempted fate.

12

INK

I sent a text to King as I jogged downstairs to the lounge. Rafa's call had been shitty timing. Although, twenty minutes earlier would have been even worse. But no matter how much I would have preferred to spend the rest of my day worshipping my woman's naked body, I wanted this crap dealt with.

Ace met me at the door to King's office and lifted his chin in greeting. "Found the bookie," he said as we walked inside.

"So you know who he owes?" I assumed.

"Yeah. Guessing you talked to Rafa?"

I nodded.

King sat at his desk with Blaze sitting in a chair next to it. Wizard and Kevlar were at the conference table with a few of our enforcers, while Ash and Echo were talking in the small sitting area on the other side of the room.

"No identity on the pro, yet?" Blaze asked.

Shaking my head, I moved to stand against the wall, too restless to take a seat. "But he got us something else."

"Uncle's location," King stated.

"Yup." After confirming, I waited silently, knowing that King would give the orders when he was ready.

After some contemplation, he looked over at Ash. "Got anything?"

"I can put him away. Permanently."

"You're one hundred percent?" King pressed.

Ash jerked his chin up and down. "Got enough to get him locked up till he's dead and buried."

Picking up on their conversation, I frowned. "You want to hand him over to the police?"

"It's the fastest way to untangle the legal shit," Ash explained. "Going to prison voids the agreement between him and Annika's parents, as well as the parameters for guardianship over her trust. If Alec disappears, she'll have to wait until he's legally declared dead. Since she's an adult, guardian abandonment no longer applies. Or she'll spend who fucking knows how long gathering all the evidence of his actions while trying to navigate a court system that moves about as fast as a fucking inchworm."

"I have some of it," Wizard interjected. "But the money trail has been a nightmare for Ace and me to document since the bookie is a dinosaur, and all the transactions were done in cash with handwritten receipts."

"Might be a dinosaur, but you gotta admit that it kept him off our radar for longer than it would have taken with anyone with a digital presence," Ace reminded him.

I ignored them, still stuck on the fact that King hadn't given me the green light to put Annika's uncle in an urn. "Am I hearing you right, Prez?" I growled. "You want me to stand the fuck down on this?"

Despite my efforts to stay calm, Cerberus picked up on my tone and lifted his head from where he lay near King's desk. He rumbled a low warning in his chest.

King's steely gaze told me I was on thin ice, so I shut my mouth and silently fumed.

"Not stand down, Ink," he finally replied. "Teach him a lesson but keep him breathing."

"Breathing," I echoed.

"Know you want to end him, Ink," Blaze spoke

up. "I get it. Anyone with an old lady understands. But if you can clear out that cloud of fury for a bit, you'll see that this is what's best for your woman."

I didn't want to be logical. I wanted the threat eliminated. Preferably through extremely painful methods. But when I'd patched, I hadn't done it so I had an army of bloodthirsty, lethal cohorts at my back. I'd joined a brotherhood, and real loyalty also meant forcing each other to see reason when one of us was spiraling out of control.

I scrubbed my hands over my face a few times, then turned to face Ash. "Guarantee me that he won't have the slightest crack in his case that could put him back on the street."

Ash's expression was dead serious. "You have my word."

"He's gonna get a hell of a surprise when he sees all the charges," Wizard said with a wicked chuckle. "Mighta added some drugs and soliciting arrests to his record by accident."

"Trust me," Ash insisted. "Every one of us would protect an old lady with our lives."

I chewed on that for a good minute, giving myself time to think clearly. "Fine."

My attention returned to my prez, who nodded in approval.

"Go with Kevlar to the armory, take whoever you need. Pick him up, teach him a lesson, then dump him where the cops will find him before he dies."

I followed Kevlar to the room where we kept some basic weapons—things we used frequently. Once we were inside, the sergeant at arms opened another inconspicuous door that led to a set of stairs. At the bottom was a much larger storage room, this one holding anything else we might want or need to get shit done. It also had another exit that led to a series of interrogation rooms.

Ace, Rebel, Kevlar, and Blaze suited up as well, then we headed to our bikes. My phone pinged, and I quickly checked the text, finding an address from Wizard. Along with a digital hotel key.

Then another message popped up.

> **KING**
>
> Forget the key. Sending in Shadow and Cruze for the retrieval. Meet them at the warehouse by the abandoned rail yard.

Fuck. As much as I hated handing over the reins to any part of this operation, I understood King's decision. Shadow and Cruze were both enforcers known for their stealthy skills, particularly in acquiring things...or, in Shadow's case, people.

I relayed the message to the men with me, then we rode to the meeting spot and waited for the enforcers to deliver my package.

Four hours later, I dropped a body bag with a barely conscious asshole zipped up inside—which made me feel a little better since I hadn't actually been allowed to kill the motherfucker—back into his hotel room.

After making sure there were drugs, illegal weapons, and other shit that would get his ass busted —metaphorically since I'd already done it physically —we called 911 and left the phone off the hook.

Blaze was leaving the motel's main office when I arrived at my motorcycle. He was carrying an empty bag that had been holding around ten grand when he went inside. "No security tape, and he'll keep his mouth shut. Might actually end up being an asset in the future if we need privacy and a hotel room."

I was about to respond when my cell buzzed in my pocket.

"It's Rafa," I explained before answering the call.

"You get your man?" he asked.

"Taken care of. And Ace had a chat with your bookmaker."

Rafa had given the bookie an order to provide us with anything he had on Alec.

"*Bene.* As for the other player, it's been handled."

Which meant they'd found the hitman and taken him out.

I exhaled a relieved breath, grateful this shit was finally done. Now, Annika and I could move forward with our life together.

"*Grazie di cuore,*" I murmured earnestly.

"There is no need for thanks, *cugino.* You might not be in The Family, but you are *familiare.*"

"So that makes us square after last time?" I joked.

"*Sì,*" he chuckled. "We are even for The Family getting you shot. But…"

I frowned. "But what?"

"Not for Sunday dinner, *babbeo.* Your *mamma* is probably already showing your woman wedding dresses."

Son of a bitch! I was gonna kill him!

Rather than waste time threatening him with castration, I hung up and raced like a bat outta hell back to the compound.

Just as I hopped off my bike and was stalking to the door of the clubhouse, a message popped up on the screen of my phone.

RAFA
Ra siamo pari.

13

ANNIKA

Matteo returned with an uncertain gleam in his eyes that made me uneasy. The breath I was holding blew out in a relieved sigh when he said, "You don't need to worry anymore. He won't be an issue for you. It's done."

There was a finality to his words. I assumed that it was better if I didn't ask too many questions about why my uncle would no longer be a problem for me. I'd given my heart to Matteo, so I felt as though I needed to trust him without any reservations.

I smiled up at him and whispered, "Good."

He must've been worried about how I'd react because the tension eased from his muscular frame, and he returned my grin. "The guy he sent after you has been taken care of by The Family, too."

My smile widened. "I'd love to thank them for the help, but I'm guessing that's a subject I should avoid if I ever meet them?"

"There's no 'ever' about it, *dolcezza*. My *mamma* will be chomping at the bit to have you over for Sunday dinner as soon as I tell her about you."

My eyes widened, but before I could ask him about it, King approached us. I flashed him a grateful smile. "Saying thank you doesn't seem like nearly enough with everything your club has done for me."

"No gratitude needed," King muttered. "We only did for you what we would for any woman a Hound has claimed. You're part of the family now, and we take care of our own."

If only my uncle—my own flesh and blood—had felt the same. Except then I might not have ended up with Matteo. Although I liked to think that we still would have wound up together if my uncle's mess hadn't forced him to bring me to the compound. Our forced proximity might've sped up our relationship, but I was pretty sure that Matteo would've asked me out anyway after he finished my tattoo. Especially since he had stolen me away from Onyx that day.

"But if you want to thank us with cobbler, I wouldn't turn it down," Onyx joked.

King shook his head and walked away while Matteo pulled me against his side and turned us toward his friend.

"I could eat some cobbler," I agreed with a smile. "Seems like the perfect way to celebrate since my uncle hated all sweets."

"I like how you think." Onyx smiled. "No tattoo memorializing him, either."

I shook my head with a soft laugh. "Yeah, unlike the one you have for your mom or the ink Matteo owes me, I'm definitely not going to do anything to honor Uncle Alec's memory. Not after he tried to end my life over money I would've happily figured out a way to give him if I had known he needed it that badly."

"Too damn sweet," Matteo muttered before his brows drew together. "Hold up...how do you know about Onyx's tattoo?"

His club brother smirked at him. "Showed it to her when she came into Hellbound and told me what she wanted."

"You motherfucker," Matteo growled, his right fist clenched at his side while he pulled me closer with his other arm.

"This finally came in, and not a moment too

soon, it seems." King tossed a brown paper bag at Matteo. "I'd like to say that getting your name on her back will help ease some of that possessiveness, but I'd only be lying."

"Took long enough." Matteo dug inside and pulled a smaller version of his leather vest out and turned it so I could see the patch on the back.

I traced over the stitching and whispered, "Property of Ink."

"Need to see you wearin' this, baby. Want to show the world that you're my old lady."

"I'd love that," I quickly agreed, turning so he could help put the vest on me.

Smoothing the front lapels over my breasts, he murmured, "Fucking perfect. Just like you."

"Perfect for you."

"Damn straight." His lips curved down slightly at the edges. "Except that you'll be leaving for college soon. Promise me you'll wear this every day while you're there?"

I shook my head. "I'm sorry, but I can't do that."

"What the hell?" he growled, his gorgeous blue eyes narrowing.

There weren't any barriers to me heading off for my freshman year anymore, but I found myself in a quandary. "I can promise you that I'll wear it, but not at school."

"Why the hell not?"

"Because I don't want to go." I took a deep breath and added, "I was doing it because I wanted to get away from Riverstone and my uncle, but now he's not an issue. And you're here. Why should I run off to get a degree I don't even want in a subject I haven't picked yet when I can stay here? With you."

"You don't have to twist my arm to talk me into it." Matteo lifted me off my feet and spun around in a circle before setting me back down again. "We can start looking for a place tomorrow."

"Or you could just move in with me?" I suggested. "Help me build new happy memories in the home that used to be full of them?"

He searched my expression for any hint of doubt. "That's what you really want?"

"Absolutely." I couldn't wait to start building a life with him there. "But if you want to live somewhere else, we totally can. I just want to be with you."

"So damn sweet," he murmured. "Which is why I couldn't help falling in love with you so quickly."

Hearing those three little words from him made butterflies swirl in my belly. "I love you, too."

"Thank fuck." He gave me a quick but hard kiss. "We'll toss our shit into the back of your Jeep and my truck so we can get a head start on moving into your place."

"Damn, Ink." Onyx clapped him on the back. "You're a kept man now."

King slapped Onyx on the back of his head, but Matteo ignored him. "You're gonna meet my *mamma* sooner than expected."

"How come?" I asked.

"Even with him gone for so many years, she still loves my father as much as the day she married him." He reached for my left hand, brushing his over my ring finger. "The ring he gave her means the world to my *mamma*, but she's always said that the day I bring the woman I'm gonna make my wife to meet her is when she'll pass it along to her new daughter."

Happy tears spilled from my eyes. "Did you just ask me to marry you in the sweetest way possible, even though it was unplanned and spur of the moment?"

"Nope," he whispered against my lips before claiming a deep kiss. "That was me telling you that you're going to be my wife. And soon."

Less than an hour later, his mom did exactly what he said. And then she helped us plan one of the quickest weddings in history. I walked down the aisle to him surrounded by my newly found family—the Hounds of Hellfire and the DeLucas—with King at my side and my best friend only a few feet in front of me.

EPILOGUE
INK

Annika was in the kitchen cooking something that smelled like my favorite dessert when I walked in the door. I grinned and sauntered behind her.

"*Ciao, dolcezza,*" I murmured as I slid my arms around her, resting my palms on her belly and burying my face in her hair. "You smell amazing."

Annika giggled and leaned back against me.

"I do? Or my cinnamon rolls do?"

After taking another deep inhale, I whispered in her ear, "Doesn't matter. They're both making me hungry."

A shiver raced down her spine, and I smirked as I pushed her hair to the side and over her shoulder. My lips glided over the soft skin of her jaw, and one of my hands sneaked under her skirt to cup her pussy over her underwear. "It drives me insane to think about anyone else smelling your delicious treats."

Annika leaned her head back on my shoulder and looked up at me. "Except I don't care what any of them think. You're the only one I'm interested in tempting."

She winked, and I couldn't help smiling at how damn cute she was.

Her lips suddenly curled down into a pout. "Besides, it's not like there aren't plenty of women out there drooling over my man. Especially when you're inking them."

"I'm pretty sure you've thoroughly staked your claim, *dolcezza*," I teased.

Shortly after we were married, I'd come into work one day to find a blown-up wedding photo hung at my station.

My wife was soft and sweet, but she turned fierce if you messed with someone she loved. I often teased her that her inner fiery Italian was showing. But truthfully, I loved when she got possessive over me. It was hot as fuck.

"Come shower with me, and I'll remind you who we both belong to." I swung her into my arms and stalked out of the kitchen.

"My cinnamon rolls!" she protested half-heartedly.

"Midnight snack," I grunted. "I'll be plenty full when I'm done eating you, baby."

Once we were in our bedroom, I went straight to the large bathroom and set her on the counter before walking over to the shower and turning the water on. Returning to her, I licked my lips as I began removing her clothes. "Then I'm going to feed my cock to that sexy mouth of yours before I fill your pussy with my come."

It was tempting to shoot my load down her throat, but I didn't want to waste any of my seed outside her womb until I knew she was knocked up.

"I made an appointment with a doctor," she blurted out.

My fingers halted, and my worried gaze flew up to hers.

"What the fuck, Annika? Why didn't you tell me you were sick?"

"I'm not," she insisted, her hands batting at mine when I tried to put her clothes back on her. "Not really."

"I'm taking you right now."

She cupped her cheeks and smiled. "Can't you think of another reason I might need to see a doctor,

Matteo? Pretty sure it's been a top priority lately, so I'm surprised you've overlooked it."

Pausing, I frowned as I tried to understand her comment. "I don't get it."

"Then let this spell it out for you." Annika smirked and held up a small white stick with a blue cap and a little window that said "Pregnant."

I read it several times before my face split with a huge smile. "Pregnant? I knocked up my woman?"

Annika nodded and returned my grin. "I figured you'd be smug about this," she laughed.

I winked at her, then lifted her off the counter and set her on her feet. After I finished stripping us both out of our clothes, I took her hand and led her into the shower. We stood under the warm spray for a few minutes, just holding each other. Eventually, I pushed her back until she was flush against the wall. Dropping to my knees in front of her, I stared in wonder at her still flat belly. "Can't wait to see you round and swollen with our baby, dolcezza."

I smoothed my hand over her stomach, then leaned in close. "*Ciao, piccolo bambino.* It's your *papà*. Be good to your *mamma* in there. And help me out by being a boy, okay?"

Annika giggled. "You wouldn't be happy with a girl?"

Her tone was amused, so I knew she didn't seriously think that.

"I'm going to need boys first in case we have any girls," I explained.

She stared at me for a moment, then drew her head back and laughed. "My big, bad biker husband is afraid to have baby girls?"

"Not afraid," I growled. "Just enlisting help. Look at you. You're fucking gorgeous, and our daughters are going to be just as beautiful. One shotgun ain't gonna do it."

I wasn't sure what she said in reply because my attention became distracted by the round swell of her hips and the blond curls between her legs. I rubbed my lips across her pubic bone, and she shivered.

Dropping my head back, I looked up into her ice-blue eyes, grinning at the fog of lust growing in them. "It's fucking hot as hell knowing you've got my baby growing in your belly," I rasped.

Pink dusted her cheeks, but she canted her head and whispered playfully, "Why don't you show me how much?"

"*Tutto per te, dolcezza,*" I murmured before devouring her until I was full.

Then she wrapped her plush lips around my

cock, and I fucked her mouth until she swallowed every drop of my come.

Still not completely satisfied, I pulled her up to her feet and spun her around, placing her hands on the wall and tugging her ass out. Then I grabbed hold of her generous hips and fucked her from behind until we both shouted with our release.

When we'd caught our breath, I cleaned us both up, dried us off, then carried her toward our bed. On the way, her stomach let out a loud growl, causing a deep laugh to burst from my lips.

"I want a cinnamon roll," she announced, sounding ravenous as she licked her lips.

"Sure, baby. Anything else?"

"Umm...olives? And...some pineapple."

I gave her an odd look as I grabbed a pair of clean boxers and pulled them on.

"Get used to it, Matteo," she teased. "It's early days. The cravings will only get weirder."

EPILOGUE
ANNIKA

Having Georgia's best tattoo artist for a husband meant I had more ink than I originally planned. And children who always had questions about them.

Lorenzo traced his finger over the first tattoo Matteo gave me. "This one's for my *nonna* and *nonno* who are in heaven, right? Your *mamma* and *papà*?"

"It sure is," I confirmed with a soft smile. "Which you already know because I've told you the story of how I met your father more times than I can count."

I tickled his side, and his boyish laughter filled the air. When I stopped, he flashed me a sheepish grin. "I know, but you say all the time that I like to ask questions."

Lorenzo had never grown out of the "why" stage from when he was three, which I lamented on a regular basis. "You have any more for me?"

"Yup." He let the P at the end pop, his smile widening. "And this one is for the day you and *Papà* got married?"

He pointed at the tattoo on my other thigh, a red heart with a heritage rose vine wrapped around it, the bloom on top, and the date of our anniversary in the middle. "It sure is. One of the best days of my life, along with when you and your sisters were born."

He tugged at the bottom of my shirt so he could see the three dates inked on my rib cage. Poking the one on the top, he mumbled, "I know that, silly. This is my birthday."

"And what a day it was."

Unlike his sisters, who had stayed in my womb almost until they had to be cut out because I was a week overdue, Lorenzo had been impatient to be born. He came two full weeks before his due date, in the middle of the night, and we almost didn't make it to the hospital in time. Which was extremely unusual for first-time mothers.

And he'd been in a rush ever since. He learned to run only a week after he took his first steps and raced his way through the rest of his eight years on this planet. Except for when he slowed down to ask questions. Lots of them.

His attention returned to my first tattoo again. "I can't wait until I'm old enough for *Papà* to ink me."

Although Mateo had no issues with breaking the law when necessary, he'd remained steadfast in his answer every time our son asked about getting his first tattoo. "When you're eighteen."

"So stupid," he muttered with a frown.

"You better not be talking about your *mamma*," Matteo growled as he walked into the kitchen from the attached garage.

Lorenzo's expression was horrified. "Of course not. I was talking about the minimum age to get a tattoo."

Matteo nodded. "Ahh, that makes more sense."

"It should because I'd never say anything bad about my *mamma*." Lorenzo glared at him. "She's the best."

"Damn straight." Matteo claimed my mouth in a deep kiss, not caring that our son was in the room.

The children were all used to our public displays of affection, and I hoped it would mean that they would be openly demonstrative toward their partners when they grew up and fell in love.

But that didn't stop our son from giving us a hard time. "Eww, *Papà*. That's my *mamma*. Take it easy."

Mateo flashed a grin at our son and wagged his eyebrows. "But she prefers it when I—"

I elbowed him in the side and muttered, "Enough."

Lorenzo pretended to gag, making me laugh.

"Okay, you two. If you have enough energy to be a pain in my butt, then you should burn it off in a much more useful way...by helping me deep clean the kitchen. It's a mess in here."

Lorenzo was willing to pitch in, but only if his sisters helped too. "Bianca! Allegra! *Mamma* needs our help."

The girls had been hosting a tea party for their dolls in the playroom, but he yelled loud enough for our neighbors to hear him. Footsteps pounded down the stairs, and the girls raced into the kitchen. At only six and four, they weren't a ton of help, but they adored their big brother and would do just about anything he asked.

While Lorenzo bossed the girls around, Matteo leaned close and whispered, "Don't worry, *dolcezza*. I'll save some energy for later when we're in bed."

I flashed him a sensual smile. "You better."

Want to learn more about the branch of The DeLuca Crime Family in the South? The series starts off with Rafa's story in The Mafia King's Stolen Fiancée!

And if you join our newsletter, you'll get a FREE copy of The Virgin's Guardian, which was banned on Amazon.

ABOUT THE AUTHOR

The writing duo of Elle Christensen and Rochelle Paige team up under the Fiona Davenport pen name to bring you sexy, insta-love stories filled with alpha males. If you want a quick & dirty read with a guaranteed happily ever after, then give Fiona Davenport a try!

Printed in Great Britain
by Amazon